Close

Michael Flay

Polar Books

First published in 1999
by Polar Books UK, Greenways, Bowbridge Lane,
Prestbury, Cheltenham, England.

Photoset by Parker Typesetting Service, Leicester
Made and printed in Great Britain by
Creative Print and Design, Ebbw Vale

ISBN 0 9536309 00

Contents

The Mad Mother 1

The Theorist 30

The Dancer 39

The Applicant 56

The Mandarins 73

The Mad Husband 79

Davros 87

The Linguist 99

At the School 108

The Queer Man 123

The Foreign Wife 129

The Mad Mother

She was living strange, giving things up, doing damage. All the while it circulated in her, how she had entitlements. She was owed this and that, her being should be financed from outside. If she made mistakes, she wasn't responsible. She pushed the pushchair through the suburb. The streets were grey with rain, the child lurched in his seat, looking like her husband. She wanted another child; he wouldn't give her one. A sullen pout began to jut. She was entitled – it was an instinct – the man was thwarting her. She would press him and goad him with her rights and wants. He was weak, lurking drunk. She'd liked his weakness as it was no threat to her; she was weak, they could trick together.

There was the letter in the hallway. The block was dismal, angular; she climbed the steps to the flat. It was all paid for, though, by the unemployment money. Her husband had had an imaginary illness, turned religious, and now was paid for. She'd go with the television man, have his baby. A great space opened in her; she could see selfish mouths opening and shutting in a black expanse, and hear a queer chuckling, female and gloaty. She'd do them down, have her revenge. But at the same time she was the sweet one, to be wanting the baby. Let others pay for it all. Her first boy was asleep in the pushchair – there it stood in the mess of the hallway, shoes scattered, old wine bottles, guitar cases. She looked at the child in cold dislike. An instinct had brought it to her. An instinct would get her another. She gave the pushchair a twitch as she passed it, so the child's head jerked against the metal. She could hurt them if she chose to.

Now she was packing; she'd leave a note she'd gone for a week's 'little holiday' – they'd planned that she could go. At the marriage guidance sessions it had been conceded this would do her good. She liked the brutality of the note, the lack of warning. This was being decisive, 'taking herself in hand'. She would keep herself up to the mark by being unpleasant to others. And she knew he was here, from the letter. Her mother, as go-between, had dropped it in. She could ring him and he'd come 'just for the time' as he put it. He was here for the filming, for the English television.

Her boy was stirring. 'A new daddy, yes, you'll have one'. Her lips were sucked in, she was self-righteous, standing up for herself as her own mother advised. She was often round at the older woman's place, complaining, twisting her face as both sat bent on a bench and the boy played alone in another room. They'd be absorbed in their problems, ramifying out the details in a high dirty kitchen where black plastic rubbish bags spilled 'waiting to be taken down', and greasy plates stood stacked by a sink. The women's eyes went sightless as they looked in at themselves, the power of vision coiling as a worm round this or that shade of consciousness or awareness. They'd been done down; their innate niceness had been taken advantage of. The boy played, hearing their voices, the rapt talk, not understanding but hearing the tones intense, self absorbed. He'd spin out the game, covering the floor with more and more objects. Sometimes when he came again the mess he'd made would still be there – the older women had no yen for housework – and then he'd add to it, old tin trains, bits of torn up paper, broken plastic cups, rotting nuts found in a drawer, a mouldy sweet. He'd push his cars through the rubbish heaped up around.

'Yes dear, it's time to have a break. Spoil yourself'. The women were in agreement. It was to here the T.V. man's letters usually came – the older woman participated in the deception of the husband as part of her project for 'spoiling'; after all, if he was jealous, then her daughter was entitled to a more peaceful receipt of mail than the noisy husband allowed. Everyone was entitled to everything, especially if no effort had to be made to get it. This was the credo.

The daughter was to be dropped off at the station. In the dusk the rain gleamed on the grey road – the women strode side by side, self-righteous, leaning forward in the drizzle, still wrapped in conversation. The child was being pushed, left out. He could see the women's faces, the lips turned this way and that, producing the words. As yet he saw no ugliness there, his world was theirs.

The car was against a dirty mesh fence below the block. Around rose the buildings of a chemical works while a high concrete bridge curved up in a half circle over a river. The landscape was grey, obscured, dead. The station rose up, soon they were saying goodbye.

'Goodbye little sweet. Make the most of the break'. Then the woman and child were up, in the train, wheeling through the rain, up the pass.

He was loitering in the entrance hall of the station at the head of the pass. He had on his Oxford college scarf, for affectation, a wax covered coat, green like an English sports car of the past, while jeans housed his slight legs. Now he fed in his credit card to a machine. This was the life, he supposed: all was paid for, he could draw as a film maker for television on a big sum. The company paid. He was smiling: how much he had. There'd be others with far less. He had put it to good use, his education, producing the bland films for the viewers; holidays in the Alps, now, for the holiday show. There'd been others: a canal ride in Scotland, mini-golf as a hobby. Now there was the itch of sexuality, livening him. She'd be coming – he'd be gone in a few days. They'd done this before. In a café he drew out a bundle of letters.

'My dearest,

I try so hard but I always have to give up what I start. First it was my school, now my marriage. I try so hard, I always fail. But I think of you who understand me so often.

Mummy was horrid last week, but this week she's paid for all my shopping. The boy is sweet now; but my husband says I'm spoilt . . .'

The letter ran on, he could relate to it. He liked to have things easy, 'stand no nonsense' in his personal life. People either took him or left him. She was the same. He liked it, that she messed everything up. He would like to as well, smear his films with cat's dung from his cottage garden, ram it in up the cassette grooves. But he needed the money. And meanwhile were these interludes. This was living the life.

They were walking. A cold white stream ran bubbling down a gulley at the side of the road, like a streak of poison. There were the usual shops for jewels and clothes; rain streaked windows revealed well-groomed assistants blank inside. He liked it, as a compliment to himself. He could run to a money machine, dial his number, come on and spend. But they liked to be non-materialist, their fiction. She moved forwards with her hair cropped short, bent in dungarees, pulling her child by the hand. She earned nothing, so a relative had paid for this holiday. She expected to ride high, be provided for, make no provision herself beyond benefit claim.

'Is this my new daddy?' The boy was curious. The woman gave a smirk, and the man from the English T.V. was titillated.

'No dear, not exactly!' The Englishman was braying, puffing at the incline. The woman affected to be an Alpinist and had phoned for a hotel on the edge of the slopes. They ran on, tossing a schnapps bottle between them at intervals, the boy pulled behind. His mother must assert herself, rise up beyond him. She had her own life to live. The man was screeching in pleasure, a high pitched screech, exclaiming at the view. He got out a little pocket camera and began to whirr it at the snow slopes.

'Film is so right, it just makes me feel.'

'Oh yes, film is good, gut'. She threw the Germanic inflexion into her English, making herself strange. She liked to give herself off as involved in the arts. She had sat naked in an attic room at her mother's, while two homosexual friends had played the saxophone. She looked like a man herself, in the chest, they'd been artists together. She relayed the anecdote. They'd been going to make a film but had drunk wine instead, and the evening had fizzled out in her mother bursting in, disturbed by the saxophones and then backing out in liberal resentment. Now they ran on dragging the boy through the powdered snow. He'd gone blank again, lapsed out into his thoughts, while they in their own fantasy were his entertainers.

'Look how he's liking it', the mother cried. He was conscious of two pairs of eyes looking at him, two mouths hanging in space, the slightly slurred speech of the woman and a waft of alcohol from her mouth, steaming. She was on fire, her words were burning in her mouth, she would burn up. He began to cry, small snivelly sobs, ugly. She eyed him sharply. 'Come on, you're not to spoil it for me. Stop spoiling it!' She raised her voice, for the last instruction, and a sharp blank deadness entered her tone, as if flat metal spoke. He didn't understand his unhappiness. He mustn't spoil it. He made himself go ordinary. The man was peering at him, slightly bent, nervous in case his evening would be spoilt by the child.

'After we ran with you, too'.

'Ran with you too'. The boy was silent now. They moved on, across a terrace, to the reception. This was how the man liked it, seeing the familiar financial sign on a counter, the slight kudos he knew would be accorded him when it was known from his passport he was a media person. The boy was to be humoured, strung along, then sex later with the mother.

The husband had turned the key. The place had a curious empty atmosphere – he saw the paper note there in the hallway.

'Oh no. Oh no, no, no, no, no.' He was melodramatic, edging with panic.

'She'll be gone. Hoity Toity'. He tried to put a brake on himself with the last phrase. 'Just a holiday, a little break.' He repeated her words in the note. Then he was dialling her mother's number, his hands scrabbly and shaken on the dial. 'You see, it'll do her good. It'll be better in the long run to have the little break. Just let her be, and you'll both be better'. The easy words came creeping and calm out of the receiver, made plausible by the confident high accent of the speaker. 'Just let her be and you'll both be . . .' It was starting up again. He crammed the receiver down, not replying. Then he was in the living room, head down, swinging with his feet. Down went the bar stools which the mother had bought them, flew across the room, cracking cups that stood in dirty heaps. She'd been on at him about the 'little baby', wanting one, another, six or seven, it was a woman's right. He had no job, but it was her right. He gave the laugh out, and cracked out at the bookshelves. They came spinning, with a twist, books on Merlin, her guides to Switzerland, covering the floor. He ground them up a little. He gathered up her dirty clothes, left scattered in heaps, put them in a rubbish bag then dumped it in the sink. She'd taken the boy off. 'Oh no, oh no, oh no.' He repeated the words like a hysteric. But at least the evening would be peaceful. He could perhaps practise his electric organ, without the carping of her voice, 'woman's right', 'another child', 'get up', and there'd be no bent twisted shape brooding on the settee. He loathed her now for her insistences. He took up the bar stool, went to the bedroom where her objects were and smashed them one by one with the stool, all round the room. Little vials of crushed cosmetics lay scattered, her packs of contraceptives were tattered.

'Yaah, Yaah' He was jeering, derisory, he rushed up and out of the door, slamming it.

It was dark, when he saw the woodyard looming outside the mother's house. He'd gone straight there. He was in the entrance hall to the old block. Dirty plaster was holed on the walls. He moved up in the dark, round the narrow wooden staircase. He'd been told a couple had lived in the top of the house who'd had to be moved to an asylum; an atmosphere of derangement smoked off the wood walls. Here was the mother's – a mess of washing lay on a dusty landing; old coats hung outside a door and his child's games were scattered around. Inside he could hear laughing, women's voices raised.

'Oh yes, she's better off out of it!'

'Who isn't – as a woman?' There came the jerky sound of drunk women. He gave a queer grimace and knocked. There was a silence. The laughter stopped in mid throw.

'Who – who is it?' The question was nervous, querulous with irritation, a social event spoiled.

'Me – your son in law'. He put the words out, cunning, with a hint of a sob. He knew he'd be asked in, out of curiosity over the crisis. The older woman liked crises. He'd give her one. But he was only partly calculating. He was beginning to be queer.

The door opened. Two women loomed at him, in expensive dresses, necklaces. On a dirty table was a joint of meat, there were empty wine bottles. He threw himself in, headlong. He was on the ground, writhing, 'Oh no, oh no, oh no'. It was indulgence, induced – the women gave shrieks of horror. One ran into the kitchen. His wife's mother began mollifying:

'Now, now, it's nothing, nothing, a little break . . .' He sprung up, sat silent in a chair. The other woman was peeping out, a little gloating.

'Come on, talk it over'. The three sat in a circle.

They were running down the Alpine slope, hand in hand. It was like a film, he thought, with the wet grasses thrusting up, and in the distance the cold bitten out peaks of white mountains. There was a crèche at the hotel, and the boy was left behind, alone there. It had been impressed on him that being alone was something a good boy had to deal with. It would please mummy for him to be left. The next day the man would be gone. They sat on a rock overlooking the ugly modern roofs of mountain houses, expensively put up. He had the wine bottle to his mouth, on holiday, the artist abroad. They'd had the sex, at night: it had been a triumph to steal in and replace the husband, and for her part there'd been the pride of standing up for herself. The experience itself hadn't been much, but still in biological process the sperm had been released, the life process, mechanical, had been enacted. He was gloating; he must be attractive to oust the husband, and she was smirky with the spoiled feeling. 'You must come to England. I have a small house there. It's a pretty place, quite near to London.'

She looked at him, her ego running high. She thought him rich, and she'd be provided for. She bent her body forward more, twisting her face against the sunlight.

'I might come. It depends how it goes here'. There came a bleeping on his mobile phone. She could hear him talking to a woman, one of the mothers of his children. They got on well together. She'd met her too, and they'd all sat round in the past, talking relationships, how triangles were acceptable these days, even crucial. She liked it, to see herself in the van of progress. He sat on the rock with the device at his ear, his slightly flabby cheeks curving, the mouth pursed in weighing alternatives, a current man with options and emotions. He swung round when the call was over, kissing her sloppily on the narrow lips. She looked like his boy – there were no curves to her form, just dead places where shape might be, flatness. She liked it, the mild slobbering, as a compliment.

The boy was waiting, not playing, in the crèche area. A bored girl, put in charge of children's activities for the day, was sitting on a stool, her nails well painted, hair groomed, pullover appropriately fitting. For herself she'd never have children. She spoke irritably.

'He would do nothing, nothing. Not even a film would he watch. He would not play with the cars'. The Swiss

German intonation was strong. The mother eyed the boy, irked. Was he going to cut up awkward, break into her life? Surely all was organised now, for a woman to have very little to do with her own children. Yet it was an instinct to have them. She hoped she was pregnant. How her mother would ask her – 'have you missed your – you know,' and how she'd be watching at herself to see. And then this man in his waxy coat, would he be the father? She wouldn't know, there'd been her husband too. It would be dramatic. She picked up the boy, and he saw the painted face come down to him as if a stoat, or sharp faced predator was coming near. But he was too afraid to cry, as if he was floating in space. He saw the red nails of the child carer swing to her lap. They reminded him of accident blood that had come on dolls with his ambulance outfit; she seemed to him to be injured.

'Look, this could be your new daddy'. The woman smiled, insensitive, and the carer looked even more bored. How disgusting it was, all this parturition and gaucheness. For herself she'd be met in a fast car when her shift was over and sped to a rich flat for pleasures. She recoiled from the boy, glad to be rid of him. And yet she had a smile for the film man, he'd got on, was in touch with the world of celebrities, selfishness and higher spending. The man bent down to the boy, playing to the role.

He was up, the husband, down the road in the rain. He'd had the talking, he'd writhed a little more first, but then the talk had come. A vague violence filled him as a result. He knew they'd felt they'd talked him round; 'all was for the best'. He gave a squeal. He was pleased to be free of her. How she'd had at him in her insane requests for this and that. He was to give her a line of babies. He was to work all week at the engineering plant, servicing heavy machines, then on Sunday go with her to the playground, on walks. She liked to moan at him, could keep her voice up for hours, complaints, laments, the accusing. It was a kind of abuse, destruction through words.

The puddles glistened – he knew he'd be down. The voices came on, remembered fragments of the bible, moral guidance. There was the face too of the marriage therapist; his health insurance had stretched to her, he'd gone with the twisted woman there. The therapist's face was framed in black loops of hair. Little eyes twinkled like a pig's while the skin gleamed cosmetically. He'd been distasteful to her, he could tell. He gave a little run on the wet tarmac.

All round the streets ran damp. The bus lit him up in a clear white light – he was exposed. The interior shone with a purple, well-cleaned gloss, impersonal. He was exhilarated, all at once. Out in the railway station, where a broad subway lined with shops, an underground street, ran he walked among the late night immigrants, Tamils, Africans, come out to drink beers on Red Cross grants. Why bother, you got a grant if you ruined your life. He had one himself. There, ahead of him, he saw a colleague. Sometimes he gave a fill-in class at a school, cheap languages. He ran on, bent round the man's back. The man was moving on, thoughtful and alone. He was startled.

'You've heard – haven't you? About her and me?' He put a slight sob in his voice at the 'her' and his eyes looked emptily up, shut in a dog's darkness, below his black hat, a copy of a singer's. The other man eyed him back, mistrustful. He suspected the man of uselessness, the capacity to fail on and on at everything, and draw out sympathy as he did so.

'No – heard what? How could I have heard?'

'She's left me. Run off with our boy. Of course it could be just for a little break'.

The poisoned interpretations of the women came into his mouth, now automatic, as if a hard sweet burst into a bitter liquid, acrid and contaminating. He went on. 'Yes, that's it – a little break – better then'. His eyes rolled as he leaned against a pillar. A policeman was staring now at the stationary men. The shout rang out loud in the emptying concourse, 'Little break! Little break', and then died away.

'I'm sorry; I'm late. And I don't really want to hear'. The other man stood back, hard against the other. He was a fool, a constant parasite. He knew he had four children back in England, a wife, all paid for as failures by somewhere else, the state.

'So fuck off then'. The victim pulled himself together, was collected, on the attack.

The teacher was walking alongside the parked cars. The mad incident had disturbed him. There were many, it seemed, who were unable to live, lurched from crisis to crisis. If you were in contact with them they pulled you down, contaminators. Big trees hung overhead in the rain. He turned in at the wooden fence. There were the railway tracks, the green carriages in the yards. The roofs ran with the rain. Orange lights lit up the drizzle. The stairs led down to a side door – the building was old, in poor condition. But all round were the renovated residences, the street was lined with cars, Swiss plated, Zurich, Bern, Vaud. This was all that was available. Inside, a wood burning stove sent out a queer heat. He stood at the low window, looking out at the scruffy garden no-one used, the public footpath beyond, then the drop, to the lines. The dark green grass by the steps was sodden, with browning leaves across the top. He was cut off in some way; the room was resonant with past inhabitants, a couple who'd left gas rings burning to heat the kitchen and stained the ceiling black, too inept to light the stove, an addict mother who'd lived there alone with three children. She'd looked out, drugged, at the rain, giving up. So why was he there, next in line?

Once he'd been in alone. A queer rap had come. He opened the door. Two children stood there.

'We're from upstairs. We've come to play'. The elder looked at him with a twisted mouth, the speech impaired. He knew the previous tenant had let them in, random; while she consoled herself in the drug her own children were given company. The children were trying to press past. They were on the escape from their own lives – he'd seen their queer mother above, leering through the curtain, heard her tirades against her husband. He pushed them back.

'She's gone. I live here now'. The children hung back, at a loss, not understanding, grimacing. The rain washed dirt from a garden where broken glass was lodged onto the path, they moved away through the running sludge. It was a place at the bottom. He'd come there through no fault; he broke even with his work, paid his way, one of the low.

The woman was sitting in the upper flat in the suburb. Outside the chemical works pushed out its vapour, and a grey rain fell.

'You see, mummy, I just can't decide – I must go to England, to be with the father. But it might not suit me there, there might be inconveniences'.

'You must do what makes you most comfortable'.

The broken women were talking themselves up.

'When I got divorced, I had to go it alone'. The words built up, ' comfortable', 'go it alone', reality was being apportioned. The boy as usual was in the outer room, left to himself as the women discussed their lives, the significance of their minutest feelings.. 'And I'm not sure who is the father'.

The mother looked admiringly at the daughter. This was the way to be, the true note to strike.

'Never mind, dearie, it's a baby, that's all that counts. You've got to take care now, not worry. There's baby to care for now. It's an instinct, isn't it?'

There came a queer beating at the door. The women crossed the dusty outer room where the child paused in mid game with a car in his hand, looking, speculating as the women passed, the tall one curving forward, the other, his mother, a smaller replica. They were playing too, perhaps. They opened the door. In the dark and round a heap of dusty coats hanging from pegs, loomed the man's face, broken in, a queer mix of the doggish emptiness and stupidity, mental disorder, aggression. 'Come in, do'. The older woman's policy was to be liberal and human to all her daughters' former husbands. She was the consoler of another ex-husband of another daughter and yet another lived below her. The ridiculousness of it all eluded her; no sense of squalid horror came either.

He came on in, twitching, sat in a chair.

'Let's talk it out'. The daughter had become the icicle princess, intact in her own rightness, responsible for the pregnancy now, and the dilemma. She gave a haughty look. He threw her a look of aggression; he would like partly to drum her into the ground – yes that was it, a little grey drum. Her brain membrane would resonate, like a tiny drum and she'd slide bit by bit into the earth. The boy looked up, curious, used to being out of it all. It wasn't worth crying as the rows left him unheard.

'You see, David, she just felt she couldn't go on. She was tired with it, you see, she had to have a break. I was just the same. I just got tired with my husband. It was the same for me, I think for all women. And you wouldn't get up on Sundays would you, to go to the playground?' This was the key point from which the case against him was made to hang. 'Well – I'd been working all week'. He'd been manipulated onto the defensive. 'Yes, but it upset her. Other men get up'.

It was a collective reference point of the family that 'other men' did many things better than the men who were actually on the spot. 'She wanted you to get up, and you wouldn't. That fact remains. And so she grew away from you.'

'Tired,' 'grew away', lit up in his mind as concepts, little fields inside which the women ran, like toy horses. He could see the toy horses move in circles.

All the time as the mother spoke his wife sat hunched on the settee. She was safe now, she'd broken out. She knew her mother would look after her, pay for her. And there was England to try. But she'd gone down already to the social security office, found out exactly how much she would get.

It was a fair sum. She'd even been allocated a social worker to advise her and get benefits on her behalf. A mother alone has to be cared for. A queer pit rocked in her being, there were spaces in herself where feelings would be in other people. Only for her there were fish-like blanks, she would be up just for herself, touching people for sympathy as she saw fit. It was as if a genetic illness had always been on her, leaving her deficient.

Suddenly he was up, pulling at the woman's hair and dragging her by it along the ground. His boot kicked up at the table and the mother's tea cup flew high. Then he simply stopped and looked emptily round the room, frozen.

'I'm pregnant. It's Garth's child – not yours. Let's have a divorce'. The mother's eyes were glowing. She could understand best this world of crisis and separation. It endorsed her – it had all happened to her and now if it happened to others she was normalised. She longed to spread out her feelings, make the world normal in her terms. The man was exulting; he disliked the twisted woman – knew that her mad insistence on another child transcended any actual man. She could care for no-one and be no-one. He eyed her warily. He gave her hair another twist. He was broken, he'd run out to the church where he worked and pray there.

'You have sinned, sinned'. He began to preach a lesson. The child hung on the edge of the settee, looking at the faces of the adults. He was used to the high words. Once his mother had rushed at the man like a bent rugger player and raised a kick at his face as he'd curved over a piece of electric equipment. He'd seen the foot fly up to hit the mouth, seen the flesh tear. There'd been blood – coming from the face. The next day he'd told his grandmother 'mummy hit daddy'. It was a big event for him, his voice had swollen importantly as he'd passed the news across. But the older woman had pushed it aside – she didn't want to hear things about her daughter like that. So it wasn't important, he knew. Only he didn't like it, to see the ugly gone look on his mother's face, her lips twisting back white and the absent animal line of the leg curving up to the blow. Now he'd seen the hair twisted, heard the voices again that grated like metal sheets, had no feeling in. He crept away to where a bag of trains was kept. He pulled off the dirty underwear the grandmother had let fall there, and began to remove the engines; he'd often done this alone. Some engines he'd named 'mama-talky train', 'hit-me truck'. He heard a door bang, the sound of steps down wooden stairs. The women lit up cigarettes, they were living their lives, virtuous.

Garth was composed. The aircraft was flying him home. He'd been the young professional man at Geneva, queueing with the rest, his bag in hand. He saw himself though as a little risqué, one who could take the alternative point of view. He made himself up, partly out of advertisements. He liked his pleasures, to put on a certain kind of cream after shaving, to maintain his need for a different woman, from time to time. Mind you, these would be friends first – he wasn't capable of licentiousness. He liked to talk, to hear himself praised and praise the woman too. Now he was replete; the Alps had shone white, he'd been nice to the boy, his relationship proceeded. The dust spiralled up in the airless tube of the plane; he liked it in this abstract space where he was with his contemporaries. He wasn't at odds; they'd be people like him, professional and getting on. London suited him, the studios. And there was always kudos, people watched television and to be associated with one involved in it was a merit. He took it all at face value. Curious, he looked back, himself at Oxford – he'd not been keen on the studying even then, had been glad to get out and into the media. Not that it hadn't been easy to get through the studies, uncritical. He thought the woman would come –his 'waif' as he called her. The plane began to curve over London; he always liked it, this return. It was inconceivable it could be distasteful. He was a punk, in his own view up against the élite but still English, superior and proud to be so. In the media he could move in his expensive coat, a conceited fantasy upon him, breaking new ground. The mediocre programmes filtered out from him and lined his pocket. He was always high on himself, addicted to his own feelings. He liked the waif – she seemed not to feel in any way, and this matched himself. He was dead: plausible, a success – but full of rottenness. He liked light reading, books with modern prestige, film theory; books that arraigned people, were judgemental, alarmed him. No-one and nothing was to be judged, least of all himself or his darling waif. He began a note:

'My dearest, darlingest, it was so lovely in the Alps – and you will soon come to me, come to me, here, to my little house. I was so interested in what you had to say about that Dutch book, *Shame is Over* – it certainly is, for who will judge us' (the woman had made a brief reference to a Dutch woman's book about giving up family life forever to be herself) 'and we are so warm. I sometimes think we are the cleverest people in the world you and I but it's our love that keeps us so'. He would post it. He felt his own cleverness sweeping in his blood, whirled out a camera to film the clouds. The click of the machine with its official T.V. markings swung heads, approval. He was one of those the world approved. He bought presents for his three children, each by different mothers – the state helped maintain them, there were grants for the women as well as his contribution. He'd had to have them, and they were so sweet. His own mother had given him brothers by two different men; it was the new way. Women often liked to hear of his new approaches; he was an honest man of tenderness, self aware: he knew he could not be orthodox (but who could, he'd ask) and knew too he could not stint on paternity and love affairs. There was a magnetism by which twisted parts draw in their way other twists of metal: there were women to respond. He'd sent letters to the Swiss girl and her mother; the husband had been tricked well. Up they'd gone, the letters, onto the dusty top of a bookcase, tucked behind an old tin where orange peel lay hardening for months. Every Sunday the woman had come, read the letter. She'd liked it, the tricking of her husband, doing him down. Her mother had been the agent, the conduit for deception. He approved of the older woman; she held free views, was for herself only, didn't take the boring line.

The teacher moved out of the small slum. He'd studied hard, got qualified. But somehow things hadn't turned out – he was here, at the base line. It was hard enough to pay the rent, feed himself, but he just did it. Only it wore him down. He'd lost his last job. He'd been temporary. The professor had ordered him one day: 'Bring me a scone and coffee at ten'. It had been a test – he'd asked inappropriate questions, not played his cards right – to see if he could be subordinate. He'd not complied; his contract hadn't been renewed. He'd been out. It was odd, he reflected now, how things hinged more on an ability to obey, humour, than to do what one was required to do as a task: it made no difference how well you taught, if there were no appropriate endorsements you'd lose out to those who made them. How common was it, that decisions, projects turned on these little humourings and collusions. He was sick of it. The mad man had failed to turn up for his cheap class. He was in the mental hospital for a week. This was the trick here, in this Swiss land; difficult feelings became objects for therapy, drug treatment. Make a mess of yourself, you got grants, treatments. Keep yourself in order, you get no help, maybe some derision for not earning enough. The world spun in strange shapes. There'd been the call, to replace the dead-eyed man. He recalled his clutching in the subway, clammy.

Outside the shops hung their windows full of wares and women moved joyless on the pavements, eyeing products. There were the fish eyes in the aerobic shaped bodies. A few might be human – others ran in preset terms, shapes moving to the music or strings of word slogans, this or that right or wrong, making you feel good or not, enjoy yourself or not, expressed, fulfilled or not – therapies hung in the background. You never knew who functioned on what chemical or treatment: who was real? But then reality was an illusion, he'd read it at the university, the thinkers had come up with the convenient fact for this time.

She had her hand on the English latch. She knew she wouldn't be staying. But she'd come to 'try' it, so she'd be seen to have done the proper thing. A queer vacillation ran in her, between acrid destruction and being seen as nice, and correct, or at least one to have pity on. He wasn't in – she knew he'd gone to work. But she disliked it, this switching of attention away from herself. Yet she liked the money, out spending in the cafés. Only there was a lodger too. To help pay the mortgage, he'd got a lodger in. She wanted him got out. He intruded on her privacy, her infinite mullings over of her 'situation', as she put it, her desire to fill the kitchen with dirty objects, heaps of her unwashed pants, smeary oil-marks round the cooker. She wanted to defile the place. She liked to seize on the man as soon as he came in from work, start the laments, the depressing complaints, the low voice and flat face intoning. It was her compulsion with all men to be so. Once she'd rushed into a man she was living with at his work, shrieking out 'Fucking work, trash it'. She disliked projects that involved consistent effort. Her special expertise was in putting the man she was involved with in a negative mood for the day – leaving him to hang in guilt. There was always an issue.

She heard the front door close. He was back. She marshalled her face into a blank, switched off mode. He was up in the conceited brightness.

'Why couldn't this baby be paid for like your others?'

He was taken aback – something wrong.

'Why, you knew how I was committed there – the public school places reserved and so on. I didn't know I'd meet you – how can I change it?'

'Why should I have less than the others?' She gave her boy a jerk; he'd been listless all day as his mother had lain on the settee and refused to play, her problems augmenting inside her in grim births. He was used to her switched off phases – the pale, dead face and refusal of contact. 'Mummy's tired, dear', his grandma had told him. 'All women get tired of their children'. So he knew he made his mother tired, her ailment was his responsibility. The man came in, caught up in the women's snare. 'New Daddy, new Daddy' – the boy jumped hopefully, but the man was intent on the dispute.

'But you knew how things were. You can live here, you're welcome too, with me. But you know I have those other children, my Grecian life. Oh waify-waif, I wrote you so'. It was true, he'd told her these things. They had been part of his appeal, exotic and a follower of the new. But now she was out for excuses to go – and he should pay. She recalled her mother, on the evening she'd left, how they'd talked. 'He's rich, mummy'.

'Well you be sure you get what you need. "What's your's is mine and mine's my own". You tell him that. Get what you need. Why, a man should provide. He'd made you pregnant'. She talked as if the woman had nothing to do with it, hadn't invited him to her country, tempted him with her boyish, ugly frame, fed into herself the biological instrument of pregnancies, rocked crouching with it inside herself. 'All men are the same – want what they can get. You get it back out of him'. The woman knew his sons were entered for expensive private educations – her own should have the same. What did practicalities matter – that there wasn't enough money left. He should find it.

Now in the kitchen she was entering her favourite element of the complaints. She could flow on in a graty dead voice for hours at a stretch.

'All you think of is money and yourself. Your own things. I'm here dead with worry, and all you can do is go to work'. She spat at his collar. 'Work'.

He eyed her back, shifty. He must've indeed done wrong to make her feel like this. He must make it up to her.

'And that lodger. I thought it would be just us'.

'But I've been earning less, lately'.

'You should have thought of me'. She was moving deeper into her own element, striking out from her dead face, effective as she was unreasonable.

She'd been out in the day, buying meat. Each day she had to have a slab of it, for the baby. There the meat lay, on the brown paper, like the inside of her womb laid bare. It made her tender for herself, as if she saw her own organ exposed. Then the vision changed, it was a meal, to keep her strength up. The pavement stretched grey back to the house; she was a long way from home, from her mother's purse. But the man was paying. She was nostalgic, a lost Swiss girl, here in the foreign place. She wanted to be back, having beers with her circle of friends in the little bar in the Swiss city centre. They'd understand her. They were there all the time, nothing to do, complaining, they'd been done down, their specialness had gone unnoticed, they'd had backgrounds that had set them at disadvantage. Large sums had been spent by their families, on schools, on making up to them for this and that, but all had been useless. They rotated at the bottom, intact in their own view. And here no-one saw her; she looked about at the rain-covered street. A few shoppers were en route home, people were at work. She was just a bent ugly figure, if seen at all, not special. Her own righteousness rose up. She had entitlements. She must get back; here frightened her. 'Yes, just work. It's dirty here; no one talks to me. I'm alone'.

'You could try to find some job, or read. You must have had things to do in Switzerland'.

She hadn't told him of the days wasted in the bar, the fog of the alcohol distractions, the mutual commiserating. Rather she'd given herself off as moving with artists, sometimes reading avant-garde German novels or feminist texts. It had been easy to keep the fantasy up in letters, or brief meetings. Now he was seeing her as vacant. It wasn't aesthetic, he felt.

The boy was creeping round the room, twirling knobs on machines, moving about objects. She left him do as he liked wherever he was. Her circle believed that parents shouldn't intervene. And often she was lying on the bed, with the difficulties in mind not knowing what he did. She longed to be paid for more, to be recognised – her emotions ran finer than other people's, she was penetrating. So she saw herself. She imagined herself as the wife of a rich businessman, with infinite spending power and nothing required. Now there was an ugly malice in the child. He had these moods lately, in which he'd break things out of the blue, twist aside for attention. Now he smeared his body against a cupboard and pulled it towards him. The drawers began to slide out. 'Look – don't do that'. The man was firm; his voice wasn't raised. The woman flew out – her hand was at the man's face, pressing it with her nails, squeezing round the mouth, and the other smacked him across the cheek.

'That's it! Speak to him like that! You can't stand children, can you? He's nothing to do with you'.

'But I thought you wanted me to be his daddy.' She twisted free. 'No – you're to have nothing to do with that. You made me pregnant. You pay.' The door slammed.

They were loving later that night. First they went to a little bar. He'd hired a babysitter. There were friends from the television. She was able to be the little punk. She'd been photographed – she told them how she'd posed for an ugliness portfolio a friend of hers was making. They went back and carried on drinking. She was turning a corner, snapping more. Suddenly she was up. She'd decided.

'I'll be going back tomorrow'. The man was relieved. He'd liked her, had been prepared to support her as the child was his. But her outbursts had sickened him. He didn't care much.

Her mother was there waiting at the airport.

'Well then, you've tried it. It's best you're sure. You're back now. And they've been ringing from social services. There's two flats for you to choose from, and they want you to go in, about the grant'. It was part of the new feminism that women alone with children should be supported, no questions asked. 'Yes, the flat's in a nice area. Lots of room. And you can have it till the boy's five'.

The daughter put on the dead look, the face of feelings turned backwards.

'I'll need driving lessons'. She'd calculated to get these from her mother. 'And England was awful – there was a lodger, and it rained. And he still wouldn't pay for public schools.'

'Never mind dearie. He was like your father. He wouldn't pay'. They were colluding, building up the fiction of women's experience.

'Oh, and David. He's in the Hopsbaum Clinic. Just for a week. To calm himself and get over it. It's better isn't it?' To be in a clinic didn't seem a disaster to the older woman. Her daughter thought of the husband in the asylum. He'd been weak and she'd made him worse. A kind of exultation arose – she'd put him there. But he'd have a job on local radio when he came out – he'd talked himself into it. The queer chorus began, in which she switched to the righteous one, was in all things justified. The fact that she'd undermined, was proof she was in the right – she'd push at men, contaminate them with herself. Only the weak ones would succumb. She hated most those who ignored her or saw her as sick; she'd like to strike up at their projects and attempts at order and bring them down into a swirl of her mad feelings and views. She settled down in her mother's flat. The boy was lying on the bed with video boxes all around. His grandmother had got in a supply. He'd spoken up.

'Mummy's happy now – back in Switzerland. She'd been crying, all the time. Second Daddy, second Daddy . . .' Here he broke off. He didn't understand. He trusted the adults to manage their own affairs. It must be that all mothers were as his own. His eyes were puzzled, but he turned to the television. He still had the child's power to switch aside from what upset him – the adults hadn't broken it yet. The screen glowed, the animated figures ran. 'Yes, it's all for the best'. She was abrupt. She really wanted to get back quickly to the kitchen, hear the details of the experience, take it all to pieces and rebuild it with comments and observations. She'd been looking forward to it, letting her feelings run loose and mad, with her daughter.

He was shouting in the subway, below the rail tracks. 'She has sinned, sinned'. There were the beer drinkers standing at ledges. His dog's eyes rolled. The teacher heard him. He'd come out of a copying shop with exercises. He was reduced to this work, life in the slum. Now he heard the mad person calling out; he knew it was the occasional colleague. They'd sat in the coffee room at the small private school. In social terms they'd been equals; defined by the job and pay. He was the same as the other. Yet his biography was not the same, in terms of qualification, achievement. The society wanted to make them the same, ignore his work, put down his worked-for qualification. He would be thrust down. He was full of anger at it all, lived with it daily. He'd seen the sick woman at the school, in the distance, known her at once as a lost cause. His colleague was lost, sick – she and him went together.

'Sinned – the lord forbade adultery – she ran off to the Alps, in the flowers – it was her little break'. The Tamils were eyeing him; what disaster was this? It was unlike their own massacre victims' reactions, perhaps he was truly religious. They were uneasy, swirled the dirty brown beer with foam on like chemical scum in a polluted river, watched. It was late again. The man began to run in and out of the pillars, making choking noises, hard to swallow. His words set up a clacking in his throat, as if he were choking. Then he stood erect. The teacher was watching at a closed sweet booth. He could see the bags inside in piles, the balloons for children suspended from hooks, foil shapes on sticks. There stood a window display across the subway of settees and chairs, priced high – he was used to observing prices and wondering who could pay them. But he just wasn't one, not a lucky one: many could. The man caught sight of the display.

'Sinners. Sinners who buy. Who work on television and buy'.

He picked up a cleaner's broom and began to beat on the glass. It was reinforced and the broom bounced off like a drum stick. He was drumming on the window. The Tamils grew restless on the stools and an old woman watched in the damp lit up air. A blue light glowed in a phone booth, put in to stop addicts injecting themselves inside. He was lit up blue as he drummed. The phrases were getting less. He was just repeating himself now. The police rang through for the ambulance. The teacher was explaining, as the man was strapped inside: 'His wife went off. But he was weak anyway'. The carriers looked at him. They didn't like the judgement, but he was foreign, didn't count. The station resumed, nothing had happened.

He was back the next week, bounced up. He'd begin at the radio. The teacher passed his wife: there she was shopping. He could see her eye him, a hate lighting up her eyes, then dropping back. She nodded; her mother was behind, carrying bags, 'all for the best, now'.

She was walking alone; the boy was left behind with her mother. The main street shop windows reflected her back at herself – she didn't look. In her mind a female fixation circulated: she was an injured princess claiming her rights. She was justified: all her moods, her acts of spite, her small meannesses, were justified because she was female. It was best not to repress what you felt – this was the family tenet – or censor it. Because of your shape between your legs you were entitled to everything. She passed into the Social Security Office. With a serious face she gave in her name, was shown to a side room.

The interviewer's hair was cut short. She was out to sympathise. Here was a woman with children who must be supported. No criticism should be made, the female was sacred. With sniffs and sad eyes an edited version of the history was given. It was exaggerated, how far in England the man had refused to help her. His suggestion that she could try to get a job was amplified to a brutality. The interviewer was all tenderness and care. 'No – it's your right. You don't have to be with the father of your baby-to-come. Why should you be?' She had no children, nor wanted any, but the right to have a child of any woman regardless of economics, her capacity to make any effort whatever, was a conviction.

'Some people think I should have an abortion'. Little tears ran in her eyes, and she made her voice falter. Certainly the teacher at her husband's school would – she remembered his pompous face, as she put it. 'Just because I can't pay'. In fact the teacher had wondered why she wanted to risk running the world over with versions of herself. Perhaps uselessness was genetic? But probably it wasn't. He was sorry for her boy. He'd not got a fair chance with such a mother.

The interviewer crossed her legs. She was smart and hung back from the physical. A queer scrupulosity lit up for her the abortion couch. She saw it with its paper towel along the seat, the stirrups. Yet as she glanced at the woman before her in part she was disgusted at her uselessness. But she was convinced – a woman should have a child if she chose. Let everyone else pay. Why not? She believed women had the right to be paid for.

'It's an instinct, you see'. The pregnant woman believed this. The interviewer looked at her sharply. She didn't share it herself, if it was one. Only she'd read in her woman's theory books that there were sacred things about women, their bodies and feelings that must never be questioned or criticised. Even hysteria was a virtuous statement, so were selfish mad claims. She'd let loose herself and then she'd had that eating disorder, warm arms round her as she'd eaten the buns then sicking up, punishing herself like a spanking – as the food came up out of her stomach and she squatted waiting for its outlet, over the bowl. This was what men did to you. She'd read men could do that too, but she pushed the information aside, no it was just women. But she liked her boyfriend to come at her – there were little locks and chains, she was the shouting one, 'no, no', then there'd be the pleasure, him straddling.

'Do you have a flat?' She was composed now.

'Yes. The Security Officer offered me a choice, up to a certain rent'.

'It's near where you lived before. You would be upset to go elsewhere?

'I like that area, yes'.

The women were endorsing, supporting each other up. The pregnant woman got up. She'd got it all – she'd been seen to be in the right. She was in the right. A mad, cocky feeling bore her up. It never occurred to her she was a failure: this was it, following the instinct. She'd buy meat again, cook it up in a little saucepan in her mother's dirty kitchen. They never cleaned there, why should they? They liked talking. She saw the meat, like abortions chopped up, in the packs. It was like eating other womens' babies. Yes that was it – she ate them up, and then they issued through her, the meat re-emerged in human form. She was glad she had a boy – he'd be brought up different to the rest. Only he was weak and she was strong, the mother, the meat was for her. It was an instinct to be pregnant. She shut out how she'd failed at the birth. She'd been in labour and had shrieked out: 'Get this thing out of me, take it out'. Her screams had startled the doctors. She'd been marked down as one to have caesareans in future, 'too unstable for natural birth'. It had been a man who'd written that. She felt the meat converting to human tissue. She wouldn't like it for her boy to be strong. She must rule. There'd be the man back in England. He'd offered to come. But she refused, had all she wanted. She had no feeling – just for comforts herself.

She got home. Her mother had taken the boy off, driving in the car, visits to relatives where he was left alone as the older woman talked things over. She had to talk them over obsessively everyday, going on and on, she'd been done down at work, or had had difficult recollections of her own divorce.

Now the meat in its red blobs was in the frying pan – she looked at it greedily, nourishment. She could see her pointed, pale face, like a fifteen year old's in the mirror - her eyes were bulging, she would burst, the emptiness, she'd been done down, emptied. Her mother came in later and the daughter had the face of the dead person, the depression had to be explored. The boy saw the blank face, switched out: 'Mummy crying' he told his grandma – 'Yes dear, she's a lot on at the moment, go and play'. His spirits were running down other people's drains. He stood, staring at the woman's face, like a fish's it seemed, bloated in a pasty whiteness, self-centred. 'Play – play with me'.

His mother swung up, knocking the glass topped kitchen table with its stains and crumbs, smashing over a beer bottle.

'You bloody little selfish boy. Little selfish rat boy – can't you see I've got problems. See how I am. Can't you . . .'

'Really dearie, don't get worked up. Think of the little one to come. How are you today, little one'. The older woman patted the stomach and spoke in a baby voice. The boy had swung to be obstinate.

'Play. Play with me'.

'Leave mummy now, she's tired'.

'But she said she'd be happy in Switzerland'.

'No, we're all depressed, dear, all depressed. That's how it is.' She believed, the older woman, it was best to be frank with children.

'Bloody hell'. The woman was up, swishing over the glass table. The objects cascaded off, the glass was cracking into three, four, large bits. The boy was watching. A hot drink fell on him and he began to scream. 'Best bandage it up, lovey'. The older woman reached for a dirty tin where she kept her medicines. The bandage had a stain of old age. The boy was screaming more quietly now. The drink had flowed mostly off his arm and the flesh was red, not too bad. A little piece of glass had got embedded, but could be got out. It was a let off. 'Yes, I know how you feel. It's best to show it'. The older woman was for her daughter now. The boy was left with his arm loosely bandaged. A look as if he understood was now in his eyes.

'Daddy, mummy, shouting. That's mummy shouting now'. The older woman waved the boy away. 'You be good, and leave your mother alone for a little while. If you love her, you'll play by yourself'. He was always being left to his own devices while crises were gone through. He wandered out onto the dirty landing where his toys were scattered – they were left to lie, from day to day. Dead plants stood in pots on a ledge. There were doors to attics. In a corner stood a drier with 'ladies things' as his grandmother called them. He eyed them with an odd fear, as if the garments had a magical power, to harm. There was a green bra, the smallest size, of his mother, and pants hung from another arm. The women put these on themselves where they were different. Why were they different? Perhaps if anyone put them on they began to cry or make scenes. There was a howling as the wind blew into an attic through a broken tile and he ran to push the door open, to get back in the flat. The door had swung firm shut and there were the voices inside, enclosed, discussing, raised, harsh. He tapped at the door, no-one came, even shouted. But the women were in the kitchen. There could be rats – he'd seen a rat in the water nearby. The long black body had slithered in with the tail behind like a worm. Somehow it might live in with the pants – a heap of them lay below the drying rack, in a bowl. Yes, they might be stirring. A terror rose in him.

'You see, love, when I broke up with my husband I had to go through it all. Just like you. And I can understand it. You hate everyone, the world. But it's easier – you can get grants'.

'More meat, mummy'. Collected now the daughter cut some from the slabs she'd fried. The older woman helped herself to some large sections. They bent together. The pregnant woman could slide in and out of disorder uncannily. There was wine on the table and they took big gulps from glassfuls each. The child's video was booming. The older woman gave a gasp.

'Where's the boy? I'd forgotten him.' She began to laugh, letting herself off. 'It was the same when you were young. Your sister got all the way to the shops by herself before I realised. Still no harm done. Best to be easy'. It was an axiom here that no harm was done by anything: spells in the mental hospital, mad shoutings, hypochondrias lasting months, all were usual. There was a low beating at the door. There was the boy, white, shaking with a pale grey face – sobs came in strange almost silent convulsions. The drier was knocked over.

'Look, he's knocked the drier over. No harm done'. The boy moved back in, miserable and shrunken. 'There. See your videos'. The two women were installed again in the kitchen. He heard the gurgle of the wine, the voices resume. He turned his face to the glow of the electric screen. A small lion was being licked by its father and mother. He felt sad, watched on, nothing else to do.

The Theorist

The man was ushered forward, into the room. It had come down to this. To survive, to have the wherewithal, you had to perform, catch a selector's eye. Whereas his impulse was to baulk them. Outside the sun shone into the gritty street, filled with cars. Inside the thin men sat behind desks, ludicrous. They would make the selection, pick someone up. Their importance was in it. Yet who would be there if the cash wasn't to be earned? He would be somewhere else.

The first man bent to him.

'You've worked in a lot of places. Why?'

The candidate eyed back.

'Contracts are temporary. You have to keep changing.'

'But why?' The thin man was surprised. 'I've never changed.' It was true, he hadn't. Where he had begun so he had stopped, a lodged stone.

The interviewee didn't want to get on, rise up. They knew it. He didn't like the theories. He was there for the cash, you had to have some wherewithal. The questions were quick – he was out of the room. He didn't stay to hear their decision. He wanted to be down on the pavement, in a café, drinking a sharp coffee. Yet he didn't want to be destitute either. This was the new spirit. The line of continuity was broken. You did things, got paid or not, sank or swam. The street was alert, full of random life. Whereas upstairs the atmosphere had been stuffy, constricted, in spite of the wide ranging theoretics.

The men were talking.

'Awful bunch this time round.' A man with a jeery

twisted lip drawled out 'No stars there. I liked the girl though. She seemed to have something.'

A manly gust of laughter ran round the room. The men were all safe, having been appointed in the late nineteen fifties, not having had to compete. They were urbane, condescending.

'Let's think it over, meet again in a week. Keep them guessing.'

The Professor was in his room like an evil bird. From him came a flow of quirks and aspersions; a pent up outrage was constantly in expression. He was the upright one, winging in the truths, the new theories. His world coiled round him like insulating tyres. Titles of books stuck out round his shelves, 'Semiotics and the New', 'Postmodern Grotesques: Dwarfs and Ideology.' His thin legs folded under his chair, sparrow like. He packed papers in his case. It was holiday time but he'd gone nowhere. 'Boys and their Uses' protruded from the leather bag. He'd try to have a boy on the way home. He wanted to get rid of a temporary person on his staff. He could imagine the boy, later, passive and white cheeked, waiting as the Romans. But now there were no baths – how Foucault had understood! He'd have to go to the convenience near the Metro. Ah, this was Paris. He swung his foxtailed scarf round his neck and put on the sharp edged black coat. How he'd sent that applicant off! He went over it again.

'Of course you realise it's rather special to live in Paris?'

'Why?' The lout had answered why, had scorned scholarship and seemed uninterested in gender studies. Why? Why? The Professor felt for the photograph in his coat pocket. A beautiful boy. He was hungering.

The applicant sat in the train, passed the flat plains of the city outskirts. He wasn't going anywhere in particular. He might end up in Brussels. There was someone he liked there, but probably it wouldn't work out. He'd just ride on. You just did things. He'd studied, but what he knew was out of key with the fashion. Its meaning was for him and a few others. He had no market value. The more people who hadn't one, the better for those who had. So the society's secret aim, undeclared, was to reduce as many people's value as it could. He would pick up temporary work as he had done before, a year's contract here or there. Nothing would be permanent, love, job, life swirled in a kaleidoscope, tiringly readjusting till you were numb.

Out of the window rain cast a grey film over the battlegrounds. Here the men had fought twice in less than one man's lifetime. The rain soaked fields revealed little; the country was restored. Yet the gas clouds had formed, under hot sun, among the beauties of the summer. Men's lungs frothed the blood.

Later the trains with the men and women had departed, on the same track bed as now, to technical death centres, experiments in human lust. It was all forgotten, not actively recalled. A little bloody brook ran in the corner of a field. The officers had been out raping. He saw his face in the mirror opposite, on the wall of the compartment. Would anyone dance on his behalf? The train carriage itself was old. It seemed to be indistinct. You were meant to be bright and know the theory, tolerant within limits others set. It didn't interest him. They had no explanation. The curious fatigue was coming up.

The Professor was in the toilet cubicle with the boy. Outside the green railing of the Metro steps loomed, he could see its outline vaguely jumping through the obscure window glass as he plunged clumsily on the youth. He wasn't feeling anything. He was clandestine, superior, a theorist. A kind of spite welled up to trick the boy. The boy looked round, wanting payment.

'I've no money. Come to my room as usual tonight'. The boy looked back, sarcastic, agreeing. Outside in the crowd the Professor was brisk. He had a seminar to present at a nearby faculty. He would be acidic, witty, sharpened by the experience, the secret man. How obscure he longed to be.

The audience was up for him. He was the latest thing, the

desired theorist. He knew how to pump the rhetoric. 'The absence of play and difference, the problematising of depressive affect, the faces of the "mente" . . . ' The speech went on, about it and about it. The audience were on their feet, cheering. This was he who had banished experience from the text. He stood alone at the podium, his eyes glazed. All was cynicism, he was well paid. What did it matter if he talked nonsense? Hadn't the greatest grown jaded and found communication impossible? The audience liked it that he wasn't heterosexual. It was his stamp of being special, his cross. It was the fad, that there was no meaning in anything and the individual had no power, his self was dead. It fitted well, this view, with the idea of cash work: if all was meaningless, well then, line your pockets, morality, concern, empathy, all illusion.

The cars packed round the statue on the tower. The figure of Napoleon looked down. The theorist moved the car wheel, eyed the dashboard. He too liked a luxurious context. Even though he liked, in theory, to explode hierarchy and privilege, for himself he liked both. As all was meaningless it was easy to concede to anything. Anyone who opposed him was an agent of reaction. His head ran with queer views he'd got across as sense. He could say anything and it would be applauded.

The man at the interview had got his goat, though. He bridled to recall the disrespect. He drove in to a wide parkland area, then into a courtyard with flats. The boy would be waiting. He'd given him a key. The lift smelt of a woman's scent. He imagined her with distaste. The boy was sitting, with music on, coming from an ugly, expensive layered unit, with perspex and lines of controls. The Professor entered unseen. Now he wanted to be cuddled by youth, treated as if the thirteen year old was his father. It would be like the Romans. His spindly body would enjoy, like an old lady eating a cream cake as she glanced at pictures of royalty. He might work it up into a theoretic point, this longing to be childish, convey it as a wish of cleverness, a radical act, in keeping with awareness of a subject's death. Which journal would he honour with his piece? They'd be queueing up for it, he knew.

'I'm clever, clever', he yelled out, throwing his bag in the air. 'Now – plaisir.' The boy was oblivious, tapping his feet to the rhythms. Suddenly a queer dislike awoke in the older man. He sat down and began to cry, sniffy sobs of ineptitude. He minced about the room, bent, in shuffly weeping. Still the boy wriggled to the pop rhythm. The professor then poured a drink and lay down to sleep. He was modern and must have his rewards. He prided himself on being able to leave his boys alone when they were playing: it made him melancholy, but it was a sacrifice his ego approved. When he woke up he rung round his colleagues on the Selection Committee. The candidate who knew most theories, had seemed most like himself, should be appointed. He was dry now, terse, the French intellectual in his own conceit. 'Yes, let's have Blackwell. He knew the points; spoke up well for sexual minorities. He knew a thing or two.' Blackwell was thin, obsequious, androgynous, author of a text, in a fashionable series, called 'Gay Balloon.' The Professor was relieved, lay back on the couch. The boy danced out in his Greek tunic with a salver of food, and hand in hand they watched Dallas, a sweetie pops evening.

The Professor was dancing. Tap tap went the cane brandished by the boy and the older man would skip from side to side to avoid it. The next day his lecture was sombre, excluding any reference to the evening's events. Writing, it appeared, had no meaning beyond its own scene. It could never be about anything but itself. Some people believed it was a window on the world, had bearing on a reality. This was ludicrous. The audience was receptive. Nothing could be accurately written. He smiled as he spoke. It was so easy to make an impression once the ball had begun to roll, of the rhetoric. He had his own public relations man now. His ethos was dominant, the Professor's, modern thinking ran on his lines. People respected him because he'd got himself set up as an object in the media's eye: anyone who got there was made, must be good, common wisdom ran.

He liked it, also, to be among the luxury fittings at the gentlemen's club in London. He'd flown in earlier that day, as he sometimes did. He'd got enough money to do as he chose. At first the men had been wary of the theorist, but gradually it was recognised that his views were as theirs, albeit more complicatedly expressed. He sat in the armchairs, next to a financier and a minister.

'So you see, what you read is nothing to do with an actual society or a real emotion. It can only be seen in terms of a fiction.'

The financier looked up.

'When my boy was at college a few years back he stirred up a lot of fuss, claiming what he read had direct bearing on how I lived. He used to row at me over it.'

'Those views were naïve, laughable now. There's no point in being a martyr.'

The manly laughter blew up. The world had changed for the better. But a current of mutual suspicion flowed between the three. Each was for himself, his own concerns and plot. How each lived, sealed up in his house or apartment was for each. They stood at an upper window looking out. There was the London street, affluent, busy, the banks close by and expensive. No-one unlike themselves was visible. You rose up and were up. Then you never went anywhere that might perturb you. The rest was sealed away like a contamination, gradually forgotten. Everything was a fiction, a game of lies, rhetoric, about itself only.

The Professor was whirling in his hotel room, with the drone of the big jets overhead, hanging in for the landing. The boy was ducking and darting and being playful. On the table were the cheap, lurid books the older man had taken to reading for pleasure, and a set of chains. He liked to feel the mesh round his neck as he was led from place to place.

Some days he'd be a bear who had to be punished for misbehaving. On the other days he'd style himself as the Nazi master. As a child he'd seen the parades in Paris, the high stepping warriors, the long leather coats of the officers, and been impressed. They'd had a dream, he'd realised later, and made the world unreal. He'd always been attracted by escapes. What did it matter?

The other men had rung down for girls and pleasure. You paid and had what you could pay for. They'd meet on the plane back to Paris. There was to be a convention at the President's palace, to discuss how culture and economics dovetailed or not. Would a particular cultural viewpoint aid economic improvements? It would be a coup if commercialism could be identified also with modernity and fashion. The girls were giggling in the financier's room and the boy was lolling on the cushions with the Professor. The youth had been with a famous singer on tour, and she'd liked to watch him move. Suddenly the Professor was blubbing again, jealous, crawling on his knees, self-humiliating, sorry for himself. He could hear the braying of the financier next door, the faint undulating of the bed, the sounds of thin ropes whipping the air. The Romans had had the baths. They were the new Romans. He felt a flush of pride emerge beneath the tears. He'd seen Goebbels in a photograph, warming up the crowds before Hitler spoke. Goebbels had written a PhD on romantic poetry. He had been a man of theory and culture, a fictionaliser. If you had met Goebbels in his suit, you would have respected him, without knowing who he was. Secretly the Professor saw himself as a philosopher manqué, lacking a cause, an outer platform. Everybody's life was unreal: life was his view of a text. He could hear the financier grunting and rustling.

Ugh – it was the applicant. There among the crowds at the airport he was sure he could see him, the man who'd been rude. He couldn't bear it, that anyone should criticise or be insolent to him. On the surface he remained unmoved by attacks, but in reality they disturbed him. How could anyone see anything differently to himself? The applicant hadn't seemed bothered by the difficulties homosexuals faced. The applicant had seemed sneery. Since the interview his face had loomed up in the Professor's dreams hatefully. Now he saw the face floating by the crushed orange stand. His blood pumped up and the financier eyed him warily, with dislike. Was he going to crack out of his image?

'Look, do you see him?'

The financier turned to scan the crowd.

'But I'd forgotten, you never saw him before. The rude man, the rude, rude man.' The Professor was shaking slightly with an effete agitation. The financier also disliked rudeness. He had even written to the papers about declining standards of behaviour on the London Underground, people eating snacks between stops.

'Is someone going to be rude?' He eyed round again. 'Some awful left wing person? I can't stand rudeness myself'.

The crowds were thicker for the check in. The theorist was uneasy. How different it would be if he could lash the people aside and proceed unimpeded. The Minister was pressing buttons on his mobile phone, speaking in a low voice to a house repairer.

'I'm having my house built on.' He explained it to the other men. 'A pricey job'.

'Pricey job' came echoed back from somewhere in the crowd. The politician was stung. None of the men liked the contact with the low. It was easier to keep up pride in their own circles. The fiction was easier to keep up, of their specialness, if unchallenged. As all their colleagues operated in terms of fantasy, it was accepted that it was best to seem, mutually, to endorse.

In the departure lounge a football team was waiting for a flight out. The players were bored at the delay. Two caught sight of the three men and called out.

'Like a game, luv?' There was a rumble of laughter round the hall. The players turned back to their cards, their broad backs in the club blazers to the men. They wouldn't go too far. Most people disapproved. The respectable men must be in the right or they wouldn't look respectable and rich. Money was the proof of anyone's worth; even better if the media attended.

The Professor hadn't heard; he'd been immersed in notes. The other two men had, but convinced themselves they'd misheard. The flight was called and the hierarchy was re-established – the respectable men's seats were plusher than the others, and a little curtain kept them hidden, élite.

The Dancer

It was at this time, men and women were separate. He climbed the stairs that curved to the upper room, with glimpses of the hardened ice on the pavements through the moon shaped glass. There was the crowd, in a circle, already – uncertain, waiting to attend, smart. A few pictures hung on the walls. She had begun the dance. Just the top of her head glowed; he would recognise it from a hundred miles off, pick it out from a thousand heads. She was standing with her head bowed, in front of the spiky wooden menhir that was opposite. It was as if her tears were falling, in the drama.

What might her tears be? What did she have to cry for? He wondered these questions, if there really was anything. She was liquid and he would like her to pour over him. But now he was objective, would give her performance the attention it deserved. The music stopped and he looked out at the road. The glimpses of the dark street, framed in the window, meant more than the amateur canvases; even the back of the supermarket car park was magical. This was the effect she had on him. Down the road would be fixed the frozen sea, the lines of ice with yellow streaks of surface melting. Her dance sent him there; the movements drew from the natural zone.

He wanted to stay, talk to her. It seemed too important, he was shy, so he went away. She eyed him quizzing, as he left. There was something between them. Only, when he spoke he distorted it. So he would go home, leave things as they were. And whatever it was she had to cry about wouldn't be his concern. And, indeed, there was probably nothing and as usual he was mistaken. He trod out onto the icy pavement. There was little for him in this cold Northern town. He was there by chance, working at random. The place wore him down and out. He was an instructor in an institute. There was a queer tiredness in him of social opposition.

He knew, too, the dancer would not be thinking much of him. She liked him, had her own path to follow. He would push his feelings down, try to ignore them. But at least the landscape was in keeping with the aim. The shut shops looked like metal cubes; people walked past in tight groups, en route elsewhere. He was used to the freezing air, by now. You had to be on your own here; everyone else was, so you should be too.

The work continued, each day trivial. His body moved in its separate enclosed physical form to the work zone. The institute was in a forest miles from the town. There were the people to instruct. It was all done for pay, without living purpose. A kiss would transfigure it all. But – he shrugged his shoulders.

He would go to the dance. The car ran across a plain where loose snow blew in glittery waves over the road. A causeway led towards a frozen sea. A queer light fell on undulating folds of ice across an empty car park to where a small ferry backed up. He was alone. A few men were visible in a room on the low bridge of the ship. He drove on. The ship was cold; the car was heaved between the pack ice as the diesel engine thumped the vessel across. It felt like a pilgrimage: what was this girl to him? Why should he care about her? Yet it was round her his feelings formed. Would she dislike the fact? But it was as actual as the ice. There wasn't much he could do about it.

He drove along a cold deserted road with woods either side. Few cars passed. It was a remote zone where his foreignness amplified. He liked the newness in himself. He was early so he'd drive across the island. The road petered out into rocks leading into the ice bound sea. A line of rusty trawlers stood on trestles. The place meant nothing, like the end of the world, a vision without meaning. All life was neutralised or slowed, frozen over and numbed. He could see beneath thin ice trapped grass; elsewhere the ice gleamed in sinister heavy folds. There were wooden houses like a Wells Fargo frontier town, on a small scale. The place scared him in its weirdness, uncanny fixed beauty, everything slowed.

She was there, in the building in the inland village. He saw her, taken by surprise, as she lay in a glass case for exhibits, on sand, folded over in a blue filmy sheath she'd made herself. Groups of spectators milled around, families, looking at pictures also on show. He felt he knew her in a way, as she lay there, the curves of her tall self speaking, the hair smoothed flat on the top of her head. For some reason he was always aware of her head. There were her hands too; strong long fingers buried in the sand. Her fingers revealed her as her words. She would crawl to wash her hair in an ice pool.

Her women friends also watched. There was a tension between them all, as if he might trespass over them as a man, harmfully. He could not help it that he wasn't a woman. What did he have to offer that wasn't female and still worthwhile? There was surely some kind of male sensitivity and gentleness worthwhile also.

The car wipers were shifting snow as it fell; a hard wind blew scuds of loose snow across the road. He was driving too fast towards the sea and getting away with it. There were risks to be taken; he'd take them at the wheel. A few dark wooden storage sheds leaned bleak at kilometre intervals in white spaces, then the road was running between flat ice, frozen water. The ferry was waiting. No car but his own went on. His feelings were down. The thick ice hung stacked along the roadway where the ferry came in, in evil folds, blocking out the life. Almost a foot thick you saw it cling to the roadway at the dock; at the sides of the road rising even thicker in layers, shining like the enclosures of the dead. Did they live here, inhabit the ice, souls of corpses like his just dead English aunts? It waited for everyone, this final end. It was like a detail from purgatory, the thick ice at the corners of the dock, projecting out in blocks over the black water where the ferry had churned its passage in. He stood by a frozen low wall, to look across at the island where the girl still was. The ferry would move along a strip of black water with the ice each side that stretched across to a low, uninviting coastline.

He would go back the next day. The ferry thumped him across the water. He drove off into nowhere, with the snow swirling thicker, the big firs set back by the road. It was hard to see at times; there was the odd feeling from the flakes on the windscreen that you were travelling backwards. He pressed on, found the place. A low building was some distance from the road. There was a pile of ice with candles burning below, at the door, set there by an artist for whom the dancer was to perform, woman for woman.

He pushed open the door. She sat at a table, just inside, already dressed to perform, casual, by herself. She smiled as he came in. He wondered what he was to her. But the affinity was there, running in his blood. He could feel her in his deepest physical self, in his stomach as it were. She looked at him gently, sensing his feelings. But she always was the wiser, she always knew. Had he been a woman he would have wanted to be her.

The small room was in the half dark; there were people at tables, gathered to celebrate the work of a woman painter. He sat by himself at a table, waiting, smoking cigarettes. Outside the snow was falling so hard it was now impossible to see the road. How could he get on back? He wouldn't care.

She had begun. She was headlong on the floor, crawling to the ice bowl, to hang her hair in the cold water, shake it, drag it back leaving a line of moisture on the ground. She was all in blue veils and folds, with a tight cover underneath: something elemental, yet a woman too, though this was incidental, unstressed. She would contract herself into arched shapes, flow in a jerky isolation as the audience watched. Some, as usual, were taken aback but were prepared to revere 'the artist' on principle. It was over. Her woman friend was speaking to her. What could he say?

Either the words came or not. The words weren't so crucial, more a cover at times for the deeper feelings. She would be vulnerable, having performed like that, to people's criticisms. She had revealed her spiritual self quite barely in the dance; there was something brave, insolent in the revelation. He could understand the impulse of naked revealing of what's felt, thought. People would come to hate her if she did it too often. But each audience was different. The hatred would be because she actually had a self to reveal, expressed something actual. She was not decorative; nothing could be further from art for art's sake than what she did. She did not fully register the risk she ran, of arousing antagonism by going further than the rest, being real. He respected her, was in collusion. He helped her into her car with the luggage: they looked at each other, and he was gone.

There was time to drive on. The snow had eased. The road twisted between trees. He didn't like it that she was no longer with him, but bowed to the necessity. Then he was out, above a frozen beach area, with more fishing boat hulls on wooden blocks, out of the water. He was alone here, with only a marine tower for company. A radar scanner rotated silently in the cold air. The edge of the land ran whitely into the ice blocked sea. There was grass below transparent ice, like an exhibit of the rare. He needed two coats as he walked. The sky was a queer pink like you'd imagine hell might show; or some mystical zone, an underworld of dream. The coast crept flatly round to a point where a works chimney, perhaps 30 miles off, blew out a plume of sheer white steam that widened, hung suspended as it rose in the windless air, uncanny. The desolation was extreme; ramshackle huts for the summer, bizarre wooden houses like models of the real stood on a low promontory, derelict now. It was like a project that had been begun, but failed in the face of the ice and subzero weather that dominated the place. The pink ethereal sky was blackening.

When he was back, he was back alone. The apartment block stood up like a castle keep, overlooking an artificial waterway that ran from a generating station to the sea. He'd stand at the window on the sixth floor, watching the thin snow fall, and the factory across the bay pumping its steam. This was the empty place, the refuge. The future was unplanned, unclear, prone to pressures and strains. How did the girl fit into it?

He turned the key to enter. There was an envelope on the mat, from the institute. He knew what it implied. The letter ran past his eyes, boring, formal, sent out of an alien world he hated, held in contempt. 'Due to policy restructuring . . .'. he ran his eyes past the crude jargon, ' your section is to be made subordinate to a new grouping. Its continuation will be subject to more clearly defined scientific and economic conditions and contexts'. So, he was to be marginalised again. It was to be expected. It was likely, reading between the lines, that the job would cease to exist at all, or contract renewal – already on a sixth month basis – would be made 'competitive' on criteria that operated against him. Here was the world beyond the dance, mixing in.

The next day there was a silent gloating in the work place, and bogus sympathy. Lip service was paid to his own area of work, but in private there was pleasure in its sidelining. Things would be more professional and scientific without it. Back in the flat he looked down at the water pumping black towards the sea, wondering what could be done? If all was shameful, how should he detach himself?

She was showing him photographs. They met for an hour

or five hours at a stretch. Now they were in a Russian restaurant. He watched her fingers, sensitive and sure, as she passed the shots. She stood on an ice boulder with a veil on; she sat in high heels on a wooden chair overlooking the frozen sea. An odd weariness also ran in him, as well as the pleasure of being with her: the work was taking him down. Also he did not know how far he could count on her and for what. Perhaps his not knowing was his own imperception.

The meeting wouldn't be a long one. She had to leave sooner than she'd planned – at the last minute she'd been rung to fill someone's classes. It was accepted between them there'd be no problems over such changes of plan. And what choice had she, if she wanted to survive in what she did? To refuse would be not to be asked again.

Only he grew tired as the hour passed. His own work had begun early that day. It seemed they were bound up in systems – he was more sceptical than she about these. She got up to go; her tall figure bent gracefully towards him and her eyes signalled that he should forgive her and that she liked him. There was something sad in himself that made their contacts sadder at this time. His work – in spite of his efforts – would be curtailed. He might have to leave the country. What there was between them should surely be allowed to grow. He didn't know what would happen.

She was busy. She kept up a life of classes, appointments relating to work. She felt she enjoyed the purposeful procedures. There would be further successes, she would be known as a dancer elsewhere. It was what she wanted.

Now the roadsides blurred past as she drove towards the town from her home; she shared a flat with a close woman friend. What might she think of it if she stopped? There was something to alarm her, looming up. The flat lands covered in snow stretched out blank on each side of the road, relieved only by the derelict black creosoted storage shacks, tilted by the winds. She hated them, these bleak stretches, empty, dull, unformed. There had to be something. And she loved her dances. Only for whom could they be performed? People told her she was getting through to audiences, expanding their hearts. But was she? She was sceptical. Could there be such expansion?

In the rich suburb she saw the cars parked in driveways, house windows decorated with lacy blind covers, all according to the home instinct, material and safe; she danced for herself. Insolently too she would dance them all to oblivion if she could. A hatred of the domestic and banal was overwhelming her. This horrible shut off suburb, the town, smug in its rich remoteness, would kill her if she had no tasks. Men could remove women's tasks, leave them empty, exposed to the white null fields. It was as if she would be eaten, abandoned to the white stillness and silence of the snow plains and forests. The place made her sick at heart.

The man would have to leave. His section of the institute was being closed down. She drove him to the airport, serious, sad. The plan was she would probably come to England soon, to study more dance. Then, she told him, they could meet. Otherwise he would be looking, in any case, for another job in Finland. She smiled as she spoke, in her own way sad. The plane lifted over the fir trees.

She started the car with a jerk. It was freezing inside; she wore two coats; a fur coat, second hand, over a black leather jacket. The car skidded onto the main road, and she flicked the tail back in, adept. A female fury against the society, herself, ran controlled and fine in her veins; she was shut in this foul snowy place. The Englishman had come close to her. She saw a group of cars bunched ahead, the thickset, material Finnish ladies at the wheels, swung vengefully past, angry still. How could she know for sure what to do? He had wanted to draw her into his conscious world, had tried also to show her himself. And she had almost seen, had wanted to see, but had not wanted to show herself so much. And yet she then had really shown him herself. What did it matter, the sexuality – with him it would have been one expression among many of their contact. The tyres slid as she spun into the parking place. She would dance herself out.

It calmed her, the high elegant room. She knew her girls, and with the tap shoes on started the routine. She would do it for herself, pass into the impersonal, self-forgetting mood. They were rehearsing for a show. Tonight she was quicker, sharper than they were, a woman in charge, talented. The mirror that ran the width of the dance studio was invisible to her – she felt the rhythm in her body as she moved. In this she could be herself, beyond relationship for the time. She had worked hard to reach this point, training and focusing her natural talent as she saw fit, regularly rehearsing, taking advantage of visits of foreign teachers to learn more, paying to take herself abroad to learn. She was in earnest.

The girls split off to take showers. She was left alone in the high elegant room, with the darkness blocking the view out. There were papers on a table – she had the school's accounts to go through. She just about broke even. Now she was strong again, having danced herself through to serious purpose. She recalled, briefly, how she had asked the man to watch her at work, how she'd wanted to show him what she'd achieved. Why had she done it? She didn't press herself further. She remembered how he'd come in to watch. What had he wanted, that she would give? Would he have been disappointed?

It was her second class. The girls came in, a little shyly, as she stood at the window looking out at the dark. She collected herself, swung friendly to face them. She looked at them professionally. The music began. She was caught up in the clear atmosphere of the room, moving over the tap floor. The dark hung at the unshuttered windows; if you pressed the glass it was ice-cold. But inside, the high well-lit room was warmed by the absorbed bodies of the women. The pleasure of movement filled the room.

There was the rhythmic sound of tapping, the energetic

swing of the feet as the warm-ups began. She was at the front of the group, facing them with the mirror behind. There was space between herself and them and she looked commanding – there was an elegant strength about her. She announced to them she would show a new routine she'd devised. She demonstrated it, absorbed in the movements, the self-forgetting display.

In the dark avenue where the two girls had their flat the letter stuck half obscured from the letterbox. In the blackness they hardly noticed it. They were caught up in a joke. Overhead the tall trees swayed icy in the night; the wind rocked them from the sea. The fir branches revealed then hid the round harsh moon that loomed queerly, too big, in the wintry dark. It was too cold to loiter in the road where the snow was packed hard and glittery. The dancer pulled out the letter. She was always curious about contacts with outside. She recognised the man's writing and her mood began to change.

'What is it? Who is it from?' Her friend was coming across, doing the tap movement again unsteady on the ice, joking, querying.

'Him in England'. She stuffed the letter down in her bag. She'd read it later. She wanted to know what he would say. He was a friend after all. Somehow it had then been beyond her to have wanted him to walk with her in the night. She knew that other women might have wanted him in the context of what she'd shared, would have been drawn in to communicate also by touch, contact. There was a sadness hanging in the trees; surely she could hear it humming in the desolate strand of phone wire between the black poles along the roadside. The place seemed dead, sterile, all at once. There were no birds in these trees, they'd all gone south.

She wanted to read the letter undisturbed. Her friend was asleep. She sat at the table, tore the envelope open.

'It seems you do matter – too much, in fact. But the whole thing is impossible, isn't it? I mean, I'm here, you're there.

Well, I don't believe it is impossible. What can we do? You'd better think about it. I will too.'

He was too direct. Only, in part, she was very pleased to have his letter. She would resist him all she could. But in the end perhaps she would not be able to resist. She hated the clichés of pursuit and giving in. The end could be long coming and perhaps he would not wait so long. But the letter gave her a fierce pride that he did care for her and in spite of the things she knew she did against him. There was a kind of tenderness in him accepting these. His directness made him easier to resist – had he been oblique she wouldn't have known what he felt. He wanted her to know, didn't want to keep her dodging in the dark of arbitrary absences, aloof periods done on purpose. In the end directness was best, like a bond that challenged. She sat for a while with the tea going cold in her cup, looking out of the window. There was nothing to see, it was night. But she knew well what was out there, snow on a lawn, a suburban house made of wood. The atmosphere rang with emptiness and seclusion. Tomorrow she had her tasks to perform, people to contact, arrangements to make. And she had a kind of advantage in knowing he wanted her.

The life with her girl-friend was what she was used to. That night as usual they shared the same bed. She lay with the back of the larger girl towards her; it was warm, intimate to be so. But she could hear the crack at intervals of the building's windows contracting as the air froze. She was tense, waiting for the crack, for the glass finally to explode in a cobweb of fault lines and jigsaw splinters. She hoped it would fold in on itself. What was it all? She'd read the letter again tomorrow.

The idea came in the morning, that she would invent a dance. She pushed the few bits of furniture to the edges of the room. Then she stood alone in the centre, spun to a sitting position. She stretched her leg out, very straight, reached far forward to pull off her sock. She was elegant, poised and perfectly balanced in the tension of the position.

He had seen her like that when he had come, rather nervously, to watch her perform. There was something sad, unexplained in him. Why had he been sometimes so nervous of her, ringing her with not much to say then tailing off? She pulled her sock off, threw it across the room. Everything was absurd, herself included. Her day should soon begin. She would go to a meeting, then rehearsals. The bedroom door closed behind her.

He was himself. He could see out of the window of his lodging from the table where he was reading. There was a shed for pigeons in a small walled area – beyond a mesh fence stretched high round an industrial yard. Inside were set coloured barrels with skull and crossbones poison stickers on. This was the storage area for waste chemicals. As yet no work had come his way, in spite of many applications. A grey drizzle fell across the dirty London sky. The council estate stretched across the acres, some houses with boarded up windows, uninhabitable, with lived in houses on each side. It was all nauseous and forlorn.

He'd get the train, forget this place. There was nothing for him here. His feelings were going down, wearing to a flatness, grinding at desire. The underground ran him past more lines of squalid homes backing onto the tracks. Then the train moved into a tunnel and the stations grew more sophisticated. Smarter people got on; men and women in business, young graduates eager for orthodox reward. The world of the council houses was seven miles up the line; here, it might as well not have existed. The voices were starting up, drawls, refined, people in charge. He sat on, hearing, seeing, with the disillusion as a brake. Who else was seeing? Who were these people, who did they think they were? How had they come to run things?

How far back was the dancer, what did she know of all this? She was better out of it all, over the northern margin. The money up there came partly from hidden, ugly societies down here, elsewhere – but the illusion could be kept up that all was separate comfort, in that country at least. Yet even from this city centre came the money to pay for the rustic summer cottages, the Finnish idylls. Rich Finns speculated on the London stock exchange, like any other Europeans. Perhaps he would go back there. He'd made inquiries. There could be something.

But now his feelings ran flat and low. He had his own projects that had nothing to do with paid work, were in opposition to it. Only he was on his own in these. He would have liked to have felt the physical weight of the girl against him. It would have made some kind of different, warmer, closer world for him, for both of them. But it was a dream, something that didn't fit with her project at that time. She was in her way right: the world is merciless if you expose yourself to it. Why should he dent her defences for the outside to come in? In relating to him more softly, physically, she would have lost momentum, weakened her struggled-for position. The society was draining away; running down in a network of cul-de-sacs and blind alleys.

He had her letter in his pocket. She would be coming to take a course at a London studio. For the while he was pleased.

He met her a few days later outside the dance studio. The street was full of men who'd been working in the city. They'd got the money, he hadn't. They'd been interested to get it, he hadn't. It was an inappropriate place to learn to dance. She came on out, tall, sardonic.

They began to walk, not saying much at first. It was all different to the northern place. He knew everything here so thoroughly, in such detail. She was animated; he was lapsed into a sharp anger against it all. He amused her – she liked his protest.

'Why do you take it so seriously? It's awful, yes, but we have our own things too'.

He looked at her, quizzing.

'This place is the root of it all'. He gestured to the passing men, the bank blocks. 'These are responsible for most of it'.

She took his arm for the first time. She was slipping out

of her habits. There was an unease that when she went back she would fall into place with them all again.

Everything was hung up in strange implication, possibility. It wasn't clear what would happen in any direction. She had had successes, was getting known more widely. They trod the pavement among the crowds. He hated this city, which was novel to her. Rich people were spilling out of a luxury store – from open bar doors he could hear the drawl of success, cash complacent. He recalled his own confinement to the rented room on the estate, the mass stale hardships there, stretching over the square miles.

He turned to concentrate on her. He loved the top of her head, and the slight awkwardness of her long fingers tucked round his arm. She was smiling to herself about something. He knew he liked and respected her more than anyone else. At least now he felt sure enough to be in his own moods with her; he did not need just to attune to hers. She liked it, when he didn't defer to her. At first that had been his failing. He had behaved to her with too much deference. It hadn't been interesting to be quite so much deferred to.

The future was open. She could do anything. She could even opt to proceed by herself, without anyone. She could easily train, perform, as a free agent. Whereas he was not impelled so single mindedly in the direction of a talent or function. He had his artistic work. But he did not believe, for himself, that a talent warranted for him exclusive attention. In some way she struck him as at risk, of being less than she could be.

They sat in a bar, talking.

'You see, it's like this. I won't get any kind of job here. I might, though, get one up north again'.

She was estimating. To her he seemed capable, had shown himself so. It was hard to believe he couldn't do just as he wanted. The adverse English conditions were inaccessible to her, except as vague outlines. Finland was easier, slightly less ruthless. She would like him to come to where she was, but obliquely. She didn't want to have charge of him. And, for his part, he didn't want to be anyone's charge. But neither did he want to see her, casual and detached, once every six months. He would have liked to see her every day, but there was no point in mentioning this.

'You should come. We'd be near'.

She was divided. In a way she wanted to be given over to him. This she did not acknowledge. It wasn't possible anyway. Her upper purpose was to succeed, to dance. This was the aim her emotional being centred on. He respected this. Only he wanted to fit in for her, somehow, not harm what she believed in.

When she'd gone he wondered again what the future could hold. He imagined her arrival in the small airport where the land cropped out flat into the sea and all around was cleared forest. It would be dark. Her friend would step forward as the passengers waited, informal, to pick their bags off the trailer. Then his imagination shut off. He would take the same route as her, nonetheless, work in the north, see her sometimes. London made him angry. All was for the pleasure, ostensibly. And yet how much pleasure was there, what kind and for whom? The sooner he left the better.

He packed his case in the upper room. A pigeon was stalking round a gulley on its shed, grey in the rain. The black mesh fence was hung with wet. The lines of housing ran like grids into the distance, the boards across the windows of some structures streaked yellow with the moisture. The zone was disconsolate, forgotten. Many who lived there were resigned. Times were hard, so, naturally they would have the worst, the worst lives, facilities, possibilities. Who cared? No-one came here voluntarily, no-one liked the place.

The train took him to the airport. As usual, after some distance the drawling men boarded. The men had bodies, were alive; their hearts presumably pumped the blood about them as they sat. Many got out at Paddington.

They'd be on their way to Gloucestershire, perhaps, their seventeenth century homes, affluence. They'd bought themselves out of the city, or sold themselves in, probably both.

He thought too much about these things. It was a relief to feel the plane lift off the English soil. He'd descend in a remoter place, where the sickness took a less familiar form, was on a smaller scale He did not know what he might find with the girl, in her direction. Something was between them all the same. He'd rung her – he could meet her at her performance in the capital when he arrived.

It was in an old building in the railway yards that she'd be performing. A fine snow was falling; he walked past the sidings where goods trucks stood, and the train to Russia was shunted. Through the window of the gallery he could see the women arranging exhibits. He would be too early if he went in now. Instead he took a sloping road up, paused to look out at the main tracks below. Now it would be time.

Inside plaster snake shapes covered a floor. There were boxes you could look in which led you via mirrors down strange pathways of sand, ice and lichen. She passed him en route to the dance, all in white, part a resurrected figure, part a wild white force. She took her place on a chair in front of three pictures, big, of lizard outlines. She would have her back to the audience. Music began, a long low note, and she leaned forward on her chair; her arms crossed in front of her and hands covered in plaster emerged from the cover of her body. They disturbed the man, watching, like a symbol of something gloomy or non-human. Then she was moving like one of the snakes, off the back of her chair, crawling into the central room. He watched her hair hang wetly down her cheeks; she was poised, drawing him in.

Bit by bit the audience was concentrating. She had this power to make them. She shook the plaster off her hand; the bits lay on the floor like random exhibits. Now she hung upside down singing in a doorway.

She was walking across the floor of the snake shapes, lifting her feet slowly, swivelling to change direction, this way and that. Then she was bracing herself along the window sill, back against the lintel. The dance was over.

She was glad he'd come. She smiled in communication across to him, while he waited for her to finish speaking to some officials. He was talking to her friend meanwhile. It all seemed very final, troubling. They sat in a side room set out like a chapel of subversion; church candles burned on alcove shelves while a wheel of wooden serpents hung from the roof. She balanced her chin on the edge of a chair, talked to him.

What was it then, this contact that took him to the ends of himself? There seemed further to go; she made him want to grow to a maximum, or see the point of a maximum existing. And she was glad to be with him. In a way they were partners, associates.

He would have to get back. There was a late train for the North. She'd stay on a few days. He wondered what would happen, later. His desire had its focus, clear.

The Applicant

The man was away, back leaving from the selection process. He could hear the slap of the train wheel on the line, see the fields in neutral squares that had no connection with himself, as little as a job. There'd be others, going back likewise.

It wasn't obvious what could happen. Something temporary, a compromise: all this was possible. What could come out of these conditions? The big houses stood now near the track, testimony to a fixed life. The men nearby were getting up, putting things into cases. He could hear the rustle of documents, see the expense of the suits and watches, the orderliness. Jordan was rising, opposite the candidate. He had no eyes for anyone. Jordan was turned inward, concentrated on the deals. His wife would have the food ready.

In the station carpark the big car waited. He turned the key, up in himself. He was exultant. The cash was earned, he'd done well. No-one else existed. The wife would be there. He wasn't sure he liked her. What was there though but his routine! There would be nothing to say between them. They hardly met. He left early, at seven, was back at eight or later in the evening. She'd have her tasks. Life went on. True, it was in the context of the objects, the rich services.

He'd been doing interviewing. He cast his mind back as he drove to how it had gone. He'd sat in the large room at an impressive desk, and he'd summed them up, the applicants. He could tell at once, by their emanation, who to choose. They had to look dedicated, normal, smart, not deviant to any degree. They'd be instruments, to further the profits. In the end that was all that counted. As he'd watched them, genial, with colleagues, he'd had no doubts. The queer thoughts hadn't come on. He'd been prone, lately, to odd images rising up – a body lying still in a weed filled ditch, a dwarf giggling at a party. But usually he was instrumental only, full of function and push. He took pleasure in turning applicants away who knew things against cash. Only belongers would do.

He knew how it would go on. Each day there'd be the car and train, the taxi through the London streets. He'd always be on the side of those who made the money. As the car approached the house drive he could see the bent head of his wife, her hair only visible. If he could run in and pull the hair up and down, see the head shake! Instead he was genial. They didn't say much. Tonight was no exception, just the food she'd cooked and television. Outside he could hear the rain beat on the quiet road and bushes.

Not much happened. All was as it should be. You saw the news items but there was no connection.

The applicant, Johnson, turned the corner by the mosque. The council houses stretched out in a long red line with a cemetery opposite. He had an upper room in one, with no cooker. The landlady didn't allow cooking. It was all he'd been able to afford when he'd moved here, for a temporary job, in the capital, a teacher. Like living in a slum zone, with derelict sites all around, there was nothing to raise up the spirits.

It wasn't his fault there was no work. He'd got qualifications, even experience. It was just that, with everyone kept on the jump, he'd no appetite for the contest. The rain ran down the pane – the upper window looked out onto a yard and a plain wall.

Somehow the television crew had got hold of his name. The programme, 'English Social Conditions', would be on later. They'd filmed his room, even the packets of food on the window sill. He hadn't liked them coming in, all vernacular and cynical matiness, just another item, but he'd needed the fee. Maybe the teaching union had given his name in.

Jordan and his wife saw the start of the programme. There was the road in the estate, the shot towards the upper room of the teacher. Jordan watched, intrigued. So this was how the low lived. The existence of such places was a useful threat, he knew – you'll end up there if you don't compete. 'If he was any good, he'd have a proper job.' Jordan believed that what an individual had was an index of his moral worth and ability. Thus, anyone 'any good' would inevitably have good trappings to match. Maureen nodded from her separate chair.

'But it's only interiors. That's the point. There aren't people in the programme. A good job not.'

'Its disgusting. He probably likes to live like that.' Jordan gave his comment out.

'Yes, they're a dirty lot, those in the public sector.' Jordan switched channels and the issue subsided.

Johnson didn't like anyone, now, and gave an unpleasant impression to the decent. One of his friends was in the I.R.A. and stored explosives. Employers sensed that he wouldn't be 'one of them'. It was early in the morning and the two men in the dark were taping the explosives to the signal cables. Then, at dawn, the wires would blow apart and a large detonation would blast any passing train. Johnson could see the lines glinting in the wet, the green of the signal light streaky on the rail. He knew it would be mostly businessmen passing on the early morning trains. His body gave little jerks of excitement. Something was broken in him. 'Blow them down down down' he hummed. The men worked on in silence, then parted in silence; he walked across a cindery area where lines had once stood. He'd been familiar with these broken up areas forever; since he'd been a boy he'd always lived in them. Even now his cash status meant he could go nowhere better.

His wife grunted as he got in; the child stirred to. She didn't know of his secret self. He heard the whumph of the detonation, then the sound of metal grind. There were some screams. He'd had a laugh, and now the horns of the services were in the night air. He wanted to mutter out nonsense words, 'Gazanee Yakabee'; nothing was real except the handing out of hard fates.

Jordan's train was cancelled. He heard about the explosion with a queer distaste. He'd never want to leave a bomb except among the low and workshy. Yes, he'd like to exterminate them. He'd got a photograph of a railway siding down which Jews had been shunted, or misfits. There was the solid terminal edifice in the picture, like a warehouse. He'd like to rid England of misfits. He would have to drive home. He knew he was handsome. He could keep track of investments via phone and computer. There was his wife's head again, visible through the glass. For a second he imagined it skewed in a noose swinging in the pantry. Her feet would tap the biscuit tin. It was odd how the thoughts came.

'Dreadful bombers lovey.'

The wife had handed Johnson over to the police. He'd been useless, no cash had come from him to her. She wanted to rise up, and all he could do was make bombs and criticise the state, go dead inside. She'd screamed at him before, tirades and outpourings, making herself breathless, to no avail. He'd just turned his head and gone out. Now she'd be free of him. He'd be in the van even now, down to the magistrate's for the first hearing. Her small heart and mind gabbled freedom. She could take her chances again. Her dirty word 'breasties' rose up and she had a vision of herself at a director's house being fondled. The baby sent up a wail and she gave the child a shove. 'Shut up. You're a bomber's boy. Yaah!' She'd put him in a nursery, get a job.

The French delegate was at Jordan's company. Monsieur Dardan and Jordan were on stools at the Covent Garden bar, with the drinks glittery before them. The bomb blast was old news, everything was the same. People were used to bombs. Nobody had noticed much what Johnson had done, ever; it had been a problem for him. More important issues were at stake. A financier was playfully biting a girl on the leg, and the champagne was cooling in the icy vases. All was a cliché, but everyone liked it. The Frenchman felt a cut above his company. He was a reader as well as a business man and liked to show it. 'You see, you don't need to believe. Our philosophers say that. You attune yourself, you make monies. You please yourself. Now philosophy and market forces have united.'

'I'm not a great one for philosophy.' Jordan was firm on this point. 'But I like to please myself. Only I exist. Everyone can do as I do. I just win, that's all.' He gave a sudden bray of laughter. 'Ya ha Ya ha. I just win.' There was a toot at the kerb. 'That'll be Maureen. Do let's go.'

The oaken table was stacked high with English food. There was a ham and pies. The Frenchman rubbed his hands. 'It's just like Charles Dickens'.

Jordan looked blank and his wife whispered, 'You know, the man on the banknotes'.

'Oh yes – the one who invented electricity. I suppose you mean the pie glaze looks electronic, even techno.' The Frenchman looked blank.

The bell rang. It was the kissogram girl. In she came, like a can-can dancer highstepping round the hall. The Frenchman began to perk up. Round she went, chucking the men under the chin, kicking like a Nazi queen. She'd been unemployed –this paid better. 'But this – c'est la jouissance.' The woman was writing the body, being a meeting point for various codes. Maureen hovered on the edge of the room.

It had been a filthy day with the poison trickling from the female vase, the revilings and illogical complainings of Miss Twisty. She'd been on at her husband in the kitchen, among the gleaming units. Now a zest springs up, to be part of the bad one's group, meat and drink in being nasty, well practised. She stands on her pedestal of rightness, Miss

Twistyclean, and all are low around her. Nothing is worthwhile – she is the creeping thing that has suffered the worst, though surrounded by money, the Monet beauty and centre of romance, kindness, run to seed. No help can be given to the desiccated self, head like a coconut, sting like a bee.

She was up and at the tart.

'Filthy beast. Awayday prostitute!' The girl jarred to a halt in mid kick. Monsieur Dardan had swung his eyes to fix on the declaiming English woman. Suddenly she leaped onto a dining chair and began to gyrate, copying the movements of contestants on a T.V. show she'd seen in Germany. She'd be Hot Chocolate, Tutti Frutti. On this, housewives and career women answered questions and stripped off for points and prizes. She'd flung off her jacket and was backing for the Frenchman to take it from her as on the show, kicking her legs in small sweeps as she did so. Later she'd back up for her bra to be unhooked.

The Frenchman brightened, began to enter the spirit. 'Bravo! Le plaisir! La jouissance!' He shouted and began to clap. The kissogram girl was smirking in a corner. Jordan was alarmed. 'Shall I get your pills, dear?' Now his wife was unbuttoning her blouse. There were flecks of foam on the edges of her mouth. 'Take me', she shrieked, and sprung from her chair for Jordan to catch her. He carried her out, struggling. Perhaps it would all help the deal to go through. He locked her in the bedroom. The Frenchman and the girl had gone. He could hear them muttering and jolting in a side room. He sat at his own table where the hams were set out. He began to carve thick pink slices, using an electric cutter, as from his wife's loins. All was in order. The striped wallpaper was overlaid with fake wood panelling in places; an open fireplace contained the brass fittings on a futuristic slab. Outside through the window he could see the large car with the globules separated on the waxy bonnet. He liked how each blob stood alone, out of contact. He heard his wife smashing objects in the bedroom, reviling him and the

'Awayday girl'. She would have to see the analyst tomorrow. He was cold, detached from it all. Idly he switched a small television on. A presenter, looking like women who worked for him, dressed cool like them, was elegantly detailing the cuts the government proposed. His spirits rose, oblique. 'Why should anything be for nothing?' he muttered. He was pleased education was to be badly hit. His own daughter had turned against him at the university a few years back. Who was it she'd said he'd been like? Someone in a book, Dombey, was that it, or a man in a wheelchair? He couldn't remember. He'd not seen her for years. A self-pitying sob came plumping out. The door burst open. His wife was in, calmed down after the tablet, dangerously cool, eternal seeming and crystal in a chemical stillness. Her eyes looked unseeing. His sob passed.

The Frenchman was back, the girl having gone and earned a good batch of ecus. He shook hands genially with Jordan. 'I thought you English were so cold. But it's been almost Parisian'. He winked at Maureen, who smirked back, a Lady Diana look. 'So the deal is on. Now let's eat.' After a few wines he was explaining Derrida to them both. His daughter studied. There was this new value free way of looking at literature. It was a bit like the old Thatcherism. Nothing matters, all is the same. At the root of all is despair. So to cover that you can do anything. He was pressing his leg closer to Maureen's under the table. She liked it, the Gallic pressure. The drug was making her free and easy. How nice it was that in France the money spirit included culture too.

'I'm afraid our daughter turned against us, during her studies. But it was fifteen years ago. The new ideas hadn't so fully come in then. We'd hoped she'd go into the City'. The mother had imagined the girl commuting in a navy suit on the train. Her hand touched Dardan's on the tablecloth. She was getting the swoony feeling. Her husband was on his sixth champagne. He was commenting. 'Now anyone can buy this. The champagne companies put up prices in the late eighties – marvellous times, who can blame them? Now they have to lower them.' His voice was slightly slurred and he began to dance, shuffling his feet. 'Market forces, ha ha!'

The two men would fly on to Paris in the morning. The car ran along the crowded motorway, crept through the approach tunnel to the airport. The men looked plausible, to be respected. The wife at the wheel was neat and rich. All was for the best. The airport facilities aped back to them what they were. All was designed for buying. Little shops solicited clients. The men stood in the special way businessmen favour in public – at ease, prosperous, with an air of superior cash power. Some companies sent their men on courses to acquire the manner; many men had it already, even from early boyhood, then imbibed at the public schools. These were the men to admire, who society had singled out as at the summit. The wife stood next to them, discreet, professional herself, in the long navy skirt and expensive jacket. Her pills were in a phial in her gold-chained handbag. It would all go on the same.

The men had gone. Now the car was back on the fast road. She was soon in the discreet avenue where trees hung and the large houses stood. The drive was familiar – the gravel sweep, then the dark oak door. Her pride was up with the drug helping. In the porch at the back a figure sat on the step. Maureen gave a start. She wouldn't go in. Perhaps it was her daughter come back. This was what she sensed. Turning, she got back in the car and drove off. She'd have lunch at the Sports Club. The younger woman moved slowly out of the garden, hearing the car. 'Still the same', she reflected. She'd been in the area for an interview and thought she'd take a chance.

Back then the students had been in the gardens talking. A pink rose had trailed up an old stone wall. There'd been the discussions, the hours of work alone. She'd realised finally that her parents had never liked her. She'd been sent to a boarding school as early as possible; before that there'd been au-pairs, mostly from Finland. Several had been fat, placid girls but could hardly take the trouble an actual mother might. Her father, alive as always to the market, had paid the minimum rate and expected maximum hours. Her mother had worked in the business, doing the deals, shining her nails blood red before the morning train. At first the daughter had accepted it. But, reading the books, her own intuition had taken wider, clearer form. Her parents had been zeros. She'd begun to work abroad, see them less and less. There'd not been much choice, about these movements. The ethos her parents brought about, sustained, meant there was a small demand for her work. Only cash making mattered. Teaching about the books ranked low.

The mother's legs spun on the fixed bicycle machine. Round she went as the dials twitched. Then the weights had to be raised and lowered. The young men assistants attentive in white T-shirts and bronzed faces gave her expensive advice. Or it might be aerobics, jerking to music in front of a shining, ego crammed mirror. In the sauna she panted out her half hour. In vain the Finnish au pairs had told her you rarely stay in for longer than five minutes. She wanted it all English style, her money's worth.

She would be spiteful, hard to please. In the beauty salon she complained about the colours of the cosmetics, had them changed then changed again, dabbed off and on. The crouching figure on the step loomed up. She hated her daughter for not playing the game. She wanted to twist and jeer in her face, like before. Her daughter was better than her so she'd do her down if she could. Why should she come hanging round? She should have stifled her in her cradle, swung her so her head cracked on the wall like the drunken yobbos did. What was a child but an impediment, an ugly thing to steal your time? She was up, the attractive woman with her own sharpnesses and appetite. She recalled the American accented lines from a TV programme about career women: 'What I do with my time and my baddy is my own affair'. Like the American lady, she had a 'baddy' to be trimmed and used. She'd liked it with the Frenchman. Who knew what might develop later, sensationalist. She'd like a troupe of maracas shaking athletes to wait on her. An old film had given her the idea. Then she came to. She was also the good woman, out to develop herself, self-righteous. She'd meant best for her daughter.

The younger woman poked her face through the window of her mother's kitchen. There she usually stood, the hag, done up like a smooth tart. Why should she care about her mother? Christine could see the way was clear to her father's room. She crept in, felt the emptiness. The place was vile to her, like a centre of illness. She liked books that boxed people into corners, pinned them to walls to reveal them, drew on the real. She would like to pin her father down also, an exhibit. He was evil, posing as a man to admire, bullying people with his money. She snatched up documents from his desk, in bundles, hurried back out, unseen.

It was easy to extinguish the glimpse of her daughter. Maureen couldn't care less. You earned the money and succeeded. That was all there was. As the psychiatric drug wore off a strange panic was building up, of something pumping inside, driving her on. A pill calmed her down. She'd watch television. It all suited her, how things were. All opposition had been cut out. No-one would oppose her. If anyone did, she ignored it, iced it up. She was the non-pareil. The queer fears had to be sluiced out with the drinks. She wanted to strip off, loll like a courtesan. The image of the Frenchman returned. She'd like to leap from the top of the stairs.

She found herself driving. It was a sunny evening, with the clouds flying in lit up tufts, a high wind on. Under the pills all had a deeper tinge, like an unreal intensity. She knew where her daughter lived. She'd call in on her, show her she was nothing. She turned up into a narrow street where the low lived. No-one was about. Her daughter would be reading rubbish, ideas, fictions. That world was unreal. If she could have her way she'd wipe it out. The door was ajar and she crept in. She would be the avenger, the social corrective. She could see Christine, in fact, in front of the mirror, preparing to go out. The feminine tasks antagonised the mother more. She peeped in, through the open door. It was a thrill to look, clandestine, like an affair. Just to peep in, make the observed sense one, and be gone. 'Horrible trash, Gaultier's bustier, panties.' The words rushed from the lips the medicaments had loosened. The girl spun round, aghast. She looked at the woman who was insulting her.

But Maureen was running the wriggly run towards the car. The daughter caught her up as she jerked the key in the lock. The older woman's face was caved in behind the outer fine form. She wanted to jet out abuse, eliminate the challenge her daughter was. The words flowed, writing her. The neurosis was breaking the organising self. The younger woman was self-righteous, a prig. Or she was a sensual princess or a prostitute. At last Maureen wrenched the key free, burst the car forward. She'd run loose, let fly. The car blasted off to the junction. Christine eyed the mother through the rear window, watched the head set like a blank bone, intent like an insect. The car was gone, roaring back to the upper zone.

Maureen was flying, blitzing in the setting sun. The pills made her up. She'd never be old, never give in. The world was for her and her kind. Her daughter was down, anyone could see that, among the public servants and no-hopers, people who had to queue for job interviews and live on temporary contracts, the rubbish folk. There were no goods worth speaking of where she lived, no upper style. She, Maureen, had her own shop at twenty, a chain of them at twenty five. She'd 'had to work hard for it though!' She gave the screechy laugh. A few fir trees poked up at the edge of a park. Those filthy Finns! She'd gone with her husband – a long flight to a place her au-pair had proposed. You got out and there were just snow, firs and flatness and drunk men on mobile phones. No-one went there. She reached for another pill to keep the panic down. A kind of scrapy noise echoed in her skull, like a scratchy whistling.

Her husband rang. Back in her neat drawing room with the Vogues on the glass table he told her how he'd have to fly on to Tunis with his new partner, Dardan. There was a deal to be struck. She was glad he was gone. On her own territory she could calm down, prepare for work the next day. She was cool now, checking stock on her visual display unit, detailing appointments. She took trouble with her hair, lingered in the bath, painted her nails. It was her favourite task to put on the red, paint out the face of her daughter she saw in miniature on each nail, a baby face.

The plane was set up for the landing, hanging over the lagoon. Jordan could see the barbed wire edge of the airfield, the dirty red and silver of the national airline planes. He knew at first when he'd landed he'd have the vestiges of Paris and London about him, he wouldn't feel in a foreign place. Then these would wear off. He might be back out by then. Now he had to queue to get in with the military police toting guns over the arrivals. Outside a dry sun lit up a dusty boulevard and a few scrappy palm trees, the leaves dusted over. He wouldn't want to stay here long. The limousine was approaching. He got in after the French man. Dardan would set everything up, he was in his hands here. A line of cars that looked damaged stood across the road – these were the cheaper taxis, with swathed Arab men sitting hot on the broken kerb nearby.

They reached the main street, pot-holed and semi-derelict at one end, though with an above ground metro terminus adjacent. Arab men clustered on the pavement holding small glasses of coffee. He noticed them with distaste. He'd always hated being abroad and Arabs were the worst of all. Still, some had money. He was here to get hold of some.

The tall block of the luxury hotel was close, near the bazaar. The street was broad, a copy of a Nice boulevard, but scruffy and with beggars, men with sores, as well as cars. They passed a line of buildings, heavily built like banks in Nineteenth Century Paris, with guards outside. Here stood a row of black cars; one had the badge of the German Economic Council on it, another fluttered the Tunisian President's flag. These were the Government offices. Dardan tapped him. 'We'll be in there tomorrow. But let's see our rooms.' A kind of glass enclosure revealed a coffee lounge with dirty waiters – or so Jordan experienced them – inside. There were many negroes and only a few women. He was disappointed. Glasses of water were set on tables. They passed into the entrance hall, like anywhere else. He was reassured now, in the usual. The room was also usual. He studied his papers. He was here with Dardan to finance another country's project; Tunis was the intermediary. It was clandestine, but there'd be good returns. There was talk also of being cut in to an oil shipping group. His blood was up for the power. He'd have to see about getting a woman in for the night. Dardan would know.

Another limousine, next day, took them to the top of the avenue. They were running then past docks on a thin strip of land – the road curved to cross a long spit cutting the water for about a mile. On one side sea spread out, on the other a broad lagoon. He felt alien, wanting the home suburb. The place had an electric charge of friction. He was uncomfortable. Now the car ran through a broken up suburb where men in headscarves sat on steel chairs on the pavement, and buildings with crumbling brown walls housed several families. Dardan was at home. 'The French once ruled here', he commented. 'This place is corrupt. The students strike and prance – the army shoots them up. It's good, it's the way. The government has to get on.'

A ruined church stood on top of a hill, the roof fallen in, where the Catholics had been driven out. The car swept into a yard where a villa stood with outhouses. Oranges grew on low trees. There was a black car already there.

With a bowing gesture of courtesy, a man in a suit with sunglasses across his face came out of the front door. They were ushered into a room with glass oak cabinets, a low table with flowers and fruit. It would be in the interests of the English company to fund the venture. Jordan knew better than to ask what it would be for, the provision of goods and capital. The deal was done and they were ushered out.

It looked like a storm was coming up. The sky was black and in the distance the sea was tossing white foam from swelling waves. Down the avenues, wide, tree-lined, of the suburbs the wind was getting up, and heavy rain began. He could see queer ruins, beyond a barbed wire fence, not like Roman relics in England, but uncouth, left alone, with no souvenir shops. The ruined shape rose up brutally in the dark. They took the coast road to see the sights – houses hung back to the beach, where their hosts urged them to stroll. Under black umbrellas they saw the concrete shacks back up to the sea; the buildings' focus was the road, the sea extraneous. On the beach were tin cans, old radios, random debris flung out by the houseowners. The visitors were meant to admire the distant sea and beaches opposite. A ferry from France crept lumpily through the swell, half obscured by spray and rain. The men in suits scrambled back to the cars.

The main street was blocked by men gesticulating, shouting. The cars turned up a side road. There was a rattle of guns and Dardan smiled. 'The windows are bullet proof.' But there came the bass whoof of an appliance Jordan could only glimpse in the upper window of a flat as men in Arab war uniforms scuttled back. The car in front was in flames in the rain, people running, old men with headbands peering out of entries. A second explosion blew open Jordan's car. Young men were running around him, dragging him out. He saw Dardan scrambled into a van, the little official also, himself pushed into another car. He was sped off through scrappy suburbs where men now wandered in the sun, back again. Jordan couldn't understand why they were in pyjamas, the women shopping in old dressing gowns – 'They're poor, that's their problem.' The captor explained, thought reading. 'But you wouldn't know, would you.' He gave Jordan a thump in the back with a metal bar. The car now ran through a scrubby wilderness with a stone aqueduct stretching along. In the distance a line of tanks had hemmed in demonstrators at a college. Jordan was led into a downstairs room in a kind of concrete hovel. A man in a denim jacket sat there. The driver nodded, 'Here's the financier.' No-one spoke. He was eyed curiously. There was no sign of the Frenchman or official.

'You come here, you lend to the corrupt, you line your own pockets, you go back to your dirty English avenue and live respected. We have informants. People in England have seen papers of yours.' The denim man was cool, assessing. Jordan had started to blub. A man with sores on his arm brought in coffees. Through his tears, Jordan felt the proximity of the low in a way that gave him physical revulsion. All his life he had tried to seal himself off. Now he was amongst it; it had broken in on him. 'Your English make a God of you, think you're nice. We know better. We blew your minister up this afternoon also.' Jordan was panting, a low throb like a machine. He'd seen it on television but the foreign places had just been fiction or else abbreviations on a visual display unit, codes for money. He'd been going to get away with it, but now this Arab student . . . It was hot underground. Where was he? He could hear a hysterical laugh faintly outside. No-one was left with him, he was alone.

He pushed the door open to find himself in full sunlight on a stretch of trampled lawn and dust. The captors were being manhandled into an armoured car by men in dark khaki uniforms. He was approached respectfully by an officer. In the distance a fume of smoke hung over a college, and he could hear cracks of fire. The sun was sharp on him and he knew he could exult. God had endorsed him and his ways, he was sanctioned. He wasn't given to religion, but now he felt his own holiness, swelling from his wallet in his pocket. The officer saluted. 'These are scum – revolutionary fools.' He pointed to the meshed windows of the van. The foreigner saw the slow motion whirl of a bloodied face, there was a twang of batons. 'We wish more in our country were like you.' The Englishman bowed, polite, the gentleman modest in face of deserved praise.

The uprising was easily crushed, and he was released with apologies from the Ministers of State. Now in his fine suit and tolerant face he looked successful; the oil agreement had also come off. The suburb looked sweet as he approached his home. His wife wasn't expecting him. He heard her as he opened the door, 'Little reading bitch loathsome fool Puritan innocent', muttering the abuse. He'd had his secretary when he got back, any averagely attractive woman would have done, anonymous, so he'd had the head taken off his success, blasted out in biological outflow. His skin was creamed up. Dardan had been less lucky, executed by his captors. But the French bank could come up with a counterpart, easy, from the new graduates, someone with tighter attitudes, not so cultured. Who wanted to hear about the books? He was humming like a top, on the high point, invincible. His wife was now asleep on the settee, tranquilised.

Christine could see the tanks on the television screen. A girlfriend was playing with her child in the park opposite. She could see the friend help the small girl up the steps of the slide, see the tiny legs reach the top. 'Thought you'd wanted me to help the Third World, darling', her father had sneered when she'd challenged him about overseas links in her younger days. Once she'd planned to murder her parents, creep in and shoot them up. But the Finnish au-pair had argued with her. 'There are thousands of them. Can you kill them all? It's not worth the trouble.' For a while she'd longed to shake their conceit, see them crumple out of the aplomb, silence their rhetoric. There'd been no way. So she'd cut loose. There were spiral worlds, intertwining but not aware of the other, or else aware in antagonism only. The unending clash of wills, aims wore her out. The world was up and sharp and for the cash, a lavish arcade of retail outlets and the main chance. If there was opposition it could be fictionalized and ignored. The spiral worlds intertwined like a toy on an executive's desk, but there was no perceived relation. She wanted to live her life. She could see the friend and child approach.

The Mandarins

The old man was riding, his white hair cut close to his head, the bicycle running on. He didn't know exactly who he was, his identity had faded. An impulse took him on, towards the hill. The pedals turned on the old machine. He'd had it all his life – as a young man he'd ridden it to college, sixty years back. He couldn't remember, except it was part of him now, like the people he lived with, two women. Was one his mother or wife? It was confused. The sun shone on wheatfields at the top of the hill, the sky was blue, uncanny, opened up to its own beyond and a burnt out stolen car stood by a gate to a radio mast.

An odd fear was in the air, as animals might sense. He was sniffing, not knowing who he was, in the old belted mac from the thirties. There'd been the teacher training college, he was perhaps close to it, back then in a straw hat. The images receded and he was on his way, jolting down a rock strewn path where clumps of thick grass grew toughly out. Two teenagers, hand in hand eyed him as he passed, a queer man in a mac, but with a shock of vital white hair, still youth in his eyes and composed face. He didn't look out of control. They watched the solid mudguard over the rear wheel jolt slightly as he curved round the incline over the bumps. They were gone on, the youth's hand under the T-shirt, feeling for the curve of the breast, the future, senses hot in the sun.

He would go where he had always gone. But he was late for the class; the boys would be lining up and the white cricket pullover and trousers he was so proud of weren't yet on. The ball was very red in contrast, strange fruit, a balloon. They were all poor, his pupils, from the lowest homes. Now it was all in the past, the school was demolished, reorganised, even rubbished as part of a system that had failed everyone it was said; his own part in it, like others of his age, had been derided as nothing and was to be forgotten. The sun gleamed off the hot banks of the lane as he free-wheeled down; there was the noise of water from a spring, the thick hedges shutting it behind. Some distant memory loomed of walking up here and meeting by chance a colleague, young families together. But it was vague, he didn't know. He felt weak, as if he would fall.

He swung the bike towards the home. There was the woman, perhaps his mother, to welcome him. She was anxious, her hands shaking. He didn't say anything, passed on in. The house was semi-detached, spacious, as old as he was. It was near where the school had been. He stopped on the threshold of a room: there was someone else there eating at a table, a middle aged woman. He held her in his stare, unable to make her out. He struck her as uncanny, giving the piercing look, her father.

He swung away, picked up a cat, moved on. There was the garden. He would walk there, he almost knew it, it could be familiar, but where were the tracks? He remembered the white steam hanging in a cutting, the summer reporting numbers 428 jutting from the locomotive smokebox, perhaps a headboard, the Cornishman, a summer seaside destination, going with his daughter. The locomotive would wind slow, blasting up an incline in the heat, the school holidays, curving in to the sea at last. Where were these people, his small daughter, gone now? An earlier time, clutching his mother: it was his mother at the gate, he knew it. The old woman watched him at the gate, now, to tell him off. He pushed past to look for his bicycle. Dimly he knew they'd shut him away if he didn't know who he was. He was trying to remember.

Some unease was in the daughter. She was watching, saw a face stare queer in the doorway. She lowered her fork to the plate, put off eating. She still lived at home, went out to work in a Government office. Nothing had come about for her. Still, she had a salary, the main thing. She could see the white hair, felt the aversion rising, the blank youthful face staring, who was she? Some attrition was wearing her away. She liked best days out with her mother.

The older woman was standing in the passage, used to the scene. There'd been the past, listening to lectures at the training college, she'd walked in a summer dress by the river after watching a cricket match, hopeful. The war had broken the hopes, lying under a table as bombs fell. Now the white haired man was watching her, piercing – if she admonished him he'd trap her arms, call her his mother, make her hands shake, pinion her. Her arms shook all the time now. Or he'd be gone, out before dawn, roaming the streets, on his bicycle. It was strange, he didn't forget how to use it, turn the pedals, balance. Now with a jerk of the head that ended the stare he was away again.

'He's always been queer'. The daughter was comfortable, leaning back. 'Do remember, years ago, when we were on holiday, he'd thought the car had that hole in it?' The car had been parked on the esplanade, over the bay where a concrete swimming pool stood among rocks. He'd forgotten how to drive, had to have the car checked for the hole. The teaching had gone on after the holiday, he'd been able to remember then. The woman was disgusted at his queerness, the grown-up daughter, how he'd spoiled everything. Teenagers had come shouting at the gate in tapered trousers and jackets with velvet collars, pointed shoes – winklepickers – and greased back 'quiffs', her mother had called them, Teds, yelling about the classes, jeers. He was a good teacher. She'd not been allowed to play with anyone. It was cold in the house, there was no central heating.

She heard a tap running. He'd be washing. Her mother sat on in the room, tired with it all. 'We'll go to those bookshops tomorrow, won't we? He goes to the day care then'. Her hand shook slightly on her lap.

He was out, cycling towards the council estate. It was small, lay at the end of his road. There was the Chinese restaurant where he'd taught the boy for nothing. He saw the red plastic sign with the Chinese letters on it. Men with long beards and pointed hats, sky blue coats lived in there, he'd seen their pictures in a book, mandarins. Across the dismal roofs of the council houses lay the hills. The school had been in the estate.

Suddenly he was tired, got off the bike, sat on the pavement. He'd go on later. People were passing into the betting shop, looked at him. There was the sound of a horse race commentary, on the wireless. He'd go to the race. It was near his school friend, a colleague's, he'd often gone there in the past, he couldn't remember why. His friend had tried to get jobs, promotions, been 'called up', as he put it, for interviews, hadn't been often successful. He'd laughed at the attempts, thrown his head back with the hissing laugh, sss, ssss. What did it matter now, the past, it had ended.

The confusion was there again. Often he came this way, to the colleague's house where he'd used to come before. Now they'd see him look up at the window in the back garden, round the corner, intent, in the mac. His bike was always left neat against the garage door at the front. In the past he'd left it against the green bank below the hedge, in the road: a policeman on a bike had knocked at the door, warned the visitor to take it in, in the dark. It was the same bicycle now with its curving handlebars and thick mud-guards, maintaining his continuity. No police rode here now, in recent years the lane was a byword for robberies: there'd been changes, he'd be gone soon, cracked and eaten like a nut. It was sometimes still the past, he was back in it. But he was ill.

The face pressed against the window, the white shock of hair loomed. If you were asleep it startled you to jerk awake and see it. No-one was in. He would go round, look in all the windows. There was the furniture, the same as in the past. He was feeling ill. He recalled there'd been a cat, a large white one, with a cankered ear and he hoped to see it, back through forty years, the Secondary Modern master and cricket coach. He sat down on the grass, below a plum tree in the garden, settled to wait. Too much had changed, the schools, the town. There was something horrible lurking, to destroy him. He wondered if he'd come by car or bicycle, he couldn't recall.

The elderly couple found him on the lawn. He went to call on them repeatedly. 'I don't feel well', he'd say, and sit in the garden with a cup of tea. He wanted to be mothered, saw women as his mothers. He'd stay ten minutes, staring as the conversation went on around him. The colleague was polite, kind, keeping up simple, normal talk as with a foreigner: 'How is your wife? And Judith, your daughter, how is she? How are your cats?' There came no reply to the questions. The man sat, let them take place around him, the words flew, he was lost. The ill feeling came back.

They saw him to the gate. There was the distant roar of spectators at the races: down a lane he rode to see the silk shirts, pink, garish colours, run over the jumps, jockeys on panting, thudding horses. He was confused, they were mandarins with beards leaping from the restaurant on war steeds. Something was frightening him.

'It's all for the best. We can't look after him here'. The wife had persisted for a year, putting up with the rushes that pinned her arms to her sides, the worry when he rode out and didn't return, the staring. The ambulance doors closed on him. The home was nearby. But he couldn't work in the garden, he wanted the bicycle. He'd run out, back. The drugs immobilised him, confused him more. The cats were gone and all the recollections were sunk in fog, like land glimpsed vague across a strip of frozen water wrapped in a band of vapour. There was now nothing coming to him.

He lay in the room with the trees of the avenue bent at the window. He'd often cycled down the road. The town in some way was his, he'd lived in it so long, but now it had changed, had no place for him, he was a nuisance. Young people to buy things were required: the pupils he'd taught had their successors, car thieves, stabbers of foreign students, truants sueing their teachers for allowing them to fail to make the grade. Some were so. The sickness swirled in him, a timely dissolution.

Outside the window was the dark; he wasn't at home anymore and the mainstay, the elderly woman, the middle aged daughter, were withdrawn, ended. Not even the instant contact of hand on fur was available or the touch of a garden cabbage leaf; all stirred in a sludge; he would withdraw. He was passing out, lying and not eating, carried about helpless, in a sling, letting it slip away, departing from the town. The grey loomed up to absorb him. The Secondary Modern school had been smashed down; once he'd run to send the cricket ball down the green – now he was gone, into the fog.

He shopping centre was thronged: it was all for the buying now, the jobs. He lay dead in the storage room at the undertaker's; to his wife he was accelerating away from her, further and further off, gone out finally from the familiar scenes, the new banal. His trajectory was refreshing to her, unfamiliar. She was glad to be drawn out with him, novel, in the acceleration away.

The Mad Husband

He was coming on down the road, decrepit and deliberately wild. But a kind of madness was in him. He'd just been to the church and his blood was up. The foreign city was around him. True, he had his place here now, his job in the factory, servicing the machines. He'd lie on his back in oil, wrenching at the screws, his flesh sometimes cut. He thought he was like a certain singer, aimed to encourage the resemblance.

Now it was raining, the street was dark. The concrete housing blocks that hung over the pavement were a different colour to those he'd been used to: small signs revealed the foreign place. A supermarket lit up to his left. He saw it vaguely, the German words on the window, not registering. He couldn't understand them all. An odd anger beat up. He was low, connected with a queer person. His wife was queer and so was he. The refrain ran in him. His own parents hadn't liked him. His father had been an officer in the army; he'd made himself in reaction a busker, a common boy. He wanted to be low, to spite them.

The road led on straight, past blocks, a wet playing field behind a mesh fence. There was nothing here to stimulate. The ordinary world closed him down. He liked it though, to be as a worker. Earlier that day he'd been sent to the locomotive yards to help with the repair of an engine. It had been cold, walking to the frost white sidings, so early, with the water frozen beside the track. The Swiss men were interrupted in their routines as they sat in the converted coach where the technical staff had their breaks by his abrupt, strange appearance. His company had sent him with a replacement part.

When he wasn't working his thoughts went up and down. He wanted to be famous, to be a musician. Mad enthusiasms would carry him along, schemes that were fantasy. Going home, now, he was working himself up. He wanted to be pure. The sermon had been on Christmas, keeping clean for it. In the foreign capital the English clergyman had swayed forwards, his middle class face pink and clear. Darkly, the mechanic, Abrams, had wanted to rush him off his rostrum, see the white robes flutter in the aisle, under the candlelight. He would replace him, address the flock as God suggested. But he'd sat on, tolerated by the Englishmen and women abroad, a worker, not of their class. He'd been put down.

He began to climb the stairs to his flat. The building was long and sharp edged, built by a bus company to house its employees sixty years before. It was a utilitarian place to look at. His wife would be there with the small baby boy. He saw her, in a dressing gown with a glass of red wine beside her. He took it all in. The baby was asleep. She looked queer to him. Her moods were bizarre at times. She might cry in self-pity over her past, which she went into in detail. She'd gone hysterical when giving birth. All at once he broke out at her.

'Drinking is unclean'. He picked up the glass in a blurred rush and hurled it at the wall. The wine ran in little streaks down the paint, the glass dropped in pieces below. The baby gave a jerk in the cot. 'Off with your clothes'. His words had an odd, absolute rhetoric, he was beside himself. He grabbed hold of the woman and they began to rotate like in a rugby scrum, banal. It was easy to rip off the gown and have hold of her ankles, drag her along. She was protesting, 'No, no, Abrams no,' but it made no difference. He was the Lord and she had slighted him. There was a grinding as a loudspeaker hit the ground. Then he came to, realised he pulled her by the feet. She was up, shrieking at him. He ignored her, put on a record. It was by the musicians he liked. 'I want tea. A pint in a glass. You know what I want'. Her foamy face poked up at him. Nevertheless she went to get it. She knew herself to be bad, repulsive. He was right to treat her as he did.

She was back, in the mood when her father had rejected her, pushed her aside. Once he'd come late from his office, pulled her out of bed, abused her, 'You're a little sicky, like your mother'. There was a constant of abuse running in the family, everyone undermining everyone else. Then, when the divorce had come through, she'd been sent to a school remote in the Alps. Only broken down people were sent there. Her self closed over in dingy selfishness. She dressed raggedly; already shrunken she cropped her hair short. She was used to a violent atmosphere of complaining, laments. Her mother would shout out viciously how her life was wasted, lie in bed with imaginary illnesses. Her father would beat and insult them all, externally the rich businessman, composed, a ski racer, daring. A self assertion rose in her like the will-to-be of a slug or big insect. She could relate to the violence with her husband.

'I'm low, I'm low'. He was calling out as the record spun in its black plastic player. They'd both spent a lot on furnishings. They'd got the mother of the girl to pay off debts he'd got back in England, so there'd be more available for this. She'd agreed, in weak complicity. She believed all were low, weak. He sat then in silence as the music pumped out. He was listening to his hero, the man he wanted to be. He leaped up, miming guitar movements. 'Filthy drinker': he aimed a kick at the girl, then ran to the door of the flat to hit his head against it. They were running like animals, in and out of the rooms, round the fittings, while the baby screamed in its cot. Something was undone in them, an instinct of control, so they issued forth in squalor. The girl flung herself on the ground hanging on his leg. She looked like a small old lady, like her mother, also wicked, lying there on the cheap new carpet. Tufts of nylon shone in the spotlight, bought new. It was like home, she was used to it, the displays and hysteria.

He was divorced himself. Back in England were a wife and four other children. He never saw them. The woman who'd wanted to separate herself lived on grants in a council house. The last child had been another man's. They'd also used to run queer, abusing and jeering at each other, husband and wife. Everyone was broken, the inner slackness was masked by the outer discipline of productive labour and jobs. He believed it, that all were the same as himself.

Usually she liked to have at him just when he came in.

'Why do we live like this? I want more money, more children. And, you lie in bed at the weekend – we should be together at the playground'. Vaguely he felt the anger rise. He was tired with the work in the pits full of sludge. Only why shouldn't he then lie in? Who was she, full of wants, ugliness? He'd knock her down, show her her place. She'd be spitting at him, throwing objects. His fist was up and still the words were coming out of her, useless, he earned nothing, never helped; he wasn't listening, just hitting. Then he'd get her later to put on the costumes, have the sex. She liked this, as if the acid interchanges made all more poignant, sharp; she could feel herself vibrate to his aggressive movements, intensified, liking the weirdness.

In the morning he got up as if nothing had happened. He was bright, going to the small kitchen to prepare breakfast. The episodes were frozen off, pent back in his mind. The baby was still asleep, his wife also. He looked at them with a smile of sentiment. They were his loved ones. He would send presents to his children in England too. The poison was out. But already it was beginning to drip back from a source inside himself, filling him up gradually.

The road was dark as he waited for the bus. The Swiss milled around, rigid faced, separate. Orange street lights glowed through the rain. As he sat a sickly scent of deodorants and cheap perfume wafted. Plans ran in his mind. He would become a highly paid performer. He could play, it was true. He would rise up in Switzerland. The words of his mother mixed in with the fantasy: 'You killed your father'. He had asked his father to help move some furniture. His father had a heart attack. He saw the man falling, slumping back over a box with the regimental drum in. He had done it. He was ostracized by his brothers. He in his turn had no sympathy. He refused to be accepted back into the family when the grief wore off. No-one had liked him. A howl of exultation filled him on the tram. He was free to be as he wanted. He might be violent, he might be gentle, read the lesson at the English church at Christmas. His wife must serve him.

The gates of the yard rose up, sharp metal bars. The rain fell into dismal puddles, the buildings were dark red brick, ugly, from the last century. But a neatly lit modern sign gave the name. It was the biggest engineers' in the land, weapon products too.

He would be working at the railway yards again. The van swung into the shed entrance. He felt simple, competent in the task ahead. The locomotive had been shunted off into a siding with an inspection pit below. He'd be by himself. He preferred this world without people. The cab was high from the ground and inside queerly spare, unpainted, all brown matt metal. He moved through to where the engines were, to check the wiring. Now he was the technician, capable. The job was an easy one. By the afternoon he was back in the works again, mending the machinery that ran the conveyor belts, lying in a thin film of wet oil, twisting with the spanner in restricted space. He could feel it coming up in him, the sense of uselessness, as he plied the tools. No-one spoke to him as he knew no German. He was left isolated, always hostile.

It was the day before the band were to rehearse. He was tense at work, moving round heavily among the machines, loping and jumpy in advance. He was perhaps building up to a period of absenteeism such as he often had. After all, he was to become the star. A fantasy operated, that this could be the case. In spite of all the evidence against – his age, his lack of contacts in the music world – he kept on with the belief he could become a millionaire star. On the walk home he was obvious amongst the Swiss: clumsy, English, he didn't fit in with the sleek dressed people in the main street. He was obstinately the jerky English workman, dressed like a lad. He gave off he favoured not thinking about appearances, but, conceited, gave his own much thought. He liked his wife to wear a dress, too, have his tea brewing when he got in. There'd have to be sex as well, at least once a day or he'd feel rejected, more often if he was especially insecure. This excited her too, like being locked up when he went out, it meant he valued her. He knew he'd have a week off work, soon; an imaginary flu was developing. Then he'd lie up at home with his records, building up to a real sickness, indulging himself. He'd make his wife run about for him in the service. Days passed, the work ran on.

He turned out of the works' gates like a prisoner released. The place was left like a dirty barracks behind. He would drink. He avoided the places where the businessmen went because of his workman's clothes, and because he didn't want to go anywhere smart. He was no-one. A low bar, with orange shaded wood, opened out. Dingy men who'd been in there all afternoon greeted him. He was having the beer. Musicians would be like this, he remarked to himself. They'd have drinks, then play. He was a musician, had his own amateur band. The baby used up money for instruments, equipment. Thoughts of being a star ran round his mind like teenage fancies. The drinks numbed him down, till he was like a beast grazing in a field, dumb and slow. Now he'd go home.

They were the same streets. He wondered what he was doing walking them. It was all a repetition. He saw the ugly wife open the door – she looked like his mother, his ex-wife, women he'd disliked. She wasn't attractive enough for him. He slapped her in the face, just like that, for welcome. The baby was crawling near her. He wanted the kid in bed so he slapped her again, lifted up the child, brusque, placed him in the child's room, closed the door, ignoring the wail. The wife was crying now, so he gave her another slap. All was as usual. But with a little wriggly swerve the woman was down the stairs, out of the door, running.

'I'll run, I'll run to mummy', she told herself. She was in a queer state, blank, liking the excitement. She was used to it, having been brought up this way. She knew her mother wouldn't be surprised to see her at the door at two in the morning. It wasn't the first time she'd gone there. The man was alone, with the record playing. He left the baby in the room, crying alone.

The wife was excited, running along the road to the taxi rank. Her mother lived on the other side of the city. She was never put out by these night visits. She expected it, that marriages wouldn't work, that violent scenes would occur. Such had been her own experience. The two women would sit up, talking for hours about their problems. Now as the taxi wipers shifted the rain off the windscreen and the lights glowed orange in the street, she was almost comfortable. The man was left behind to nurse his own feelings and she was away, with all the privileges of someone who'd been hard done to.

The car twisted through a brief forest. She got out, winding between scrap cars that stood in rows in a dirty yard, towards a small block, run down. Her mother lived at the top of this. She rattled up the familiar stairs. How often she'd climbed here in states of hysteria and poured out in the room at the top. She knocked and was let in. The mother was all sympathy, putting an excusing view on everything her daughter had done.

'Of course he's mad, my little darling. All men are. My husband was too'. Both women were gratified to be proven right, to find the men defective. It made it easier for them to be confirmed in the superiority they anyway felt.

They settled down with coffees and talk. At first the

mother wondered about her daughter's baby but it was all right to have run out without it. 'They tyrannise you, the babies. Why, when I was young, I used to leave you by yourself and go out with my husband. You were just six months. I bet you cried' – here she gave her daughter's arm a squeeze. 'But you're all right now, aren't you?' The daughter simpered in reply.

There came a sudden beating at the door and a slight splintering round its hinges and lock. The door didn't budge. Outside came a man's voice, whinnying in pleas mixed with aggression. The women looked at each other and the older one turned the key. Abrams stood holding the baby in silence, handed it to his wife. The child looked round curiously, not understanding, even amused. Then he ran in, the father, threw himself loping around the room, began to twist. 'I'm vile, I'm vile', he cried as he rocked from side to side. The baby was watching, his birdy eyes peeping in interest, absorbing the atmosphere.

The scene was familiar. It had happened several times before. All the people in the room, save the baby, seemed to need it, to like to bring it on. The atmosphere of distorted emotions, intensities, thickened, impregnating the walls, ready to emanate out again. Abrams was sobbing on the ground and a queer gleam was on his wife's lips. Here was her victim, floored and at her mercy. He'd done it to himself. The older woman was in charge, supervising with advice. It was admitted, then, the husband was someone with problems. The wife exulted; she was not alone in having severe defects. The baby switched his eyes round the room, waiting to be brought up.

Davros

The big Swiss hotel was round them all. They stood at the bar eyeing the women. There were several who had gone in for this to happen. The men were in suits, comfortable, easy – the women in short skirts and dresses, displayed. It was the sort of hotel where your car is collected for you. Davros was up, in talk. He owned several of the blocks around.

There was a furtive air of sex excitement in the room. One woman's skirt was high on her thighs and her tights were lurid, shiny, with silvery designs round the ankles. The men had seen such garments advertised in shop windows in the mainstreet. They wanted some queer and lurid outcome. But there would be talking first, no doubt. Outside the road curved in front of the station – the eyes of bus passengers would be caught by the flags on poles, the nineteenth century grandiose style of the façade. They were inside, the men, amongst those who had made it. The city was built up and maintained by such people, property dealers, big shop owners, commercial directors. About ten was the group of the richest.

The women moved and the men watched. They'd all been shopping for the styles: now was the arena for display. Davros moved till he was in a position to see as much of the woman's legs as possible. Here was an enjoyment. He was easy, standing loose, on the watch. The woman positioned herself, so she was easier to be seen; he could even see the seam of her gusset, he realised, blended in as it was with the black of the nylon. He liked it, to be aware of how the woman packaged herself. He needed the additional thrust of excitement from unusual, forbidden items, glimpses from odd angles.

Outside the rain made the street black. The shoppers were milling past the hotel windows in separate lives. Davros had inherited money when younger, and with an astute eye for what would sell in property had bought up many apartments, houses, resold them. Prices were high, here in Switzerland. He liked to think up the details, see to the layout of kitchen cupboards, have the fittings futuristic but sound. This was what some women liked him for, identifying his eye for house detail with taste itself. He liked it, to take up with different women, sometimes picking on difficult cases, to test his powers. Women's breasts today were a source of pleasure, to see and have. But latterly he had found himself blasé in his seductions. Now his pleasure was to egg the woman on, to reveal herself in public. The woman in the soft leather chair, opposite, for example, was stretching her legs more, revealing their length, discreetly tugging down her pullover to keep it tight. He took in all this as he chatted.

'I see Fritz has bought a challenger yacht for the Murten lake. But he got a bad bargain there. Ernest told me . . .' The murmur of manly laughter rose up. All round the hotel the shopping streets homed in on the square it was sited in. The big department stores were there tightly, with their display counters and assistants and gaudy packaged goods. One of the men owned the largest of these. Through the hotel window he could see cowed figures pass, men in shabby coats.

'Scumbag poor types! Not got a clue.' The men gathered discreet, laughing, looking out at the pavement, easily superior.

It was for the pleasure they worked, the evenings with girls, the expensive display. Their penises were sheathed in paper francs, their ejaculations might glitter as heaps of one franc coins. The women enjoyed the feel of the money brushing their bodies, airing them off. To Rosemary the man was a hero if he had cash; he could not be pushed around, he could pay. And he could decorate himself and her with the best that could be bought of outer style. It was also fun to lie on the bed in exotic underwear, perhaps a bodice like the one she had seen in a video of a singer the previous night, with a thong at the back.

He was in the car, conscious of the sheen of the girl's legs beside him. He would have liked to stop the car there in the queue of rush hour traffic and stroke these. In one sense, what did it matter if neither cared? Why shouldn't this enjoyment happen? Only he knew she would not permit this. The game, Davros knew, was to appear uninterested until later; at the moment there was the undercurrent to explore of her being conscious of his interest and allowing it. He wanted to drive out madly, smash into the cars ahead. Why should he be thwarted in his approaches? On the left rose up a block he owned. Between them he and the men he'd just left owned much of the city.

Ordinary people were waiting to cross the road at lights. Rosemary was immune now, in contact with a leader, she felt. Her will was to be apart from the earning side of reality. In herself null, she became someone in so far as she was in the presence of money. And this man was quite young, well-fitted out in his clothes. She liked it, that his accessories were well-chosen. She wanted to feel his hands on her flesh, the sense of her clothes falling to the ground. But such moments were brief; for the most part the liaisons consisted of being out, in expensive places, being luxurious. It was like living in an advertisement. Unfortunately sometimes feelings intruded, intervening on the glossiness. It wanted something more, to make it all really easy and good.

Herr Stackli liked the new secretary. She was temporary, from an agency. Her skirt was short, her figure to his liking. She seemed to take an interest in him. For sure, he knew he was interesting. He took her into his confidence with the deals, took her to meetings where strictly speaking he didn't need a companion or assistant. He could show off to the others that he had this kind of helper. He wanted to push things further. In him was an empty sense that there needed to be more, that he was no-one. The offices were well equipped, the money earned from property sales was huge enough, at home there was a wife, even children. He could have all he saw advertised. At the end of it, though, he felt himself small, nowhere. In his head ran lists of figures, petty tastes for this and that, childish preferences for certain kinds of food, furnishings. Certain things were banned from reflection, like left-wing politics or anything 'artistic', apart from the art of appearance which he could buy up anytime. He liked to be impulsive.

'Let's close the office, go to Zurich to buy you some clothes. You could have what you liked.' The secretary looked at him, afraid for the moment. She was drawn in, by part of her which corresponded. Thinking in small terms, she could see the bags with Designer labels on them, feel the new materials with herself inside them. She wanted to be someone, so why not the boss' prostitute? What did it matter who the man was? Besides, this one had succeeded, had the power to buy. She was impressed by his possessions. Was it not better to have the touch on herself of an important man? It would be like a power for her to use.

He saw she was drawn in, moved towards her. He was practised. The outer door could be locked at the press of a button. He wanted to have his revenge on the world again and again. His hand was slipping between her thighs to the receptive zone he knew all women had. She didn't care, for the time being. It was life to her, in her inexperience. She felt his hand below her pullover, going over the straps of her underclothes. It was all impersonal. He was pressing against her in his trousers. Then, suddenly, he was stopped by his own climax. She looked at him, surprised, from her chair. He would make her one of them, the closed group. A queer smirk of satisfaction was on him, and he drew her skirt down with an air of ownership.

The pair approached the men assembled at the hotel bar. Her eyes were up, now, alert, to better herself. Someone else might want her, buy her things. Why work, why type things out, when there was this world of long lunches, drinks, clothes shopping? She would be bought along with the furnishings. To give herself away, her, Angela, feel the men wanting her, any men so long as they had commercial power. This man was now her supreme gratification. She felt as if they were all eyeing her body, assessing her. Their behaviour was gentle, respectful. She knew it was an act that complemented their lust. They were all locked into its repetition, non-developing.

There was nowhere to go, once the repetition set in. The men were daily the same, the offices, the deals, the routines of money making. Once a system was set up, it took no intelligence to run it. Setting it up involved cunning, no more. As Davros had said: 'it just keeps on coming in, the cash.' Then the counterpart was the meals, the girls. The flesh grew blasé, seeking more sensation, getting killed off. The girl could feel the damp sweet patch on her tights where the man had pressed on her. It was her trophy, to be ignored. Now she was up, humming, in the warm, expensive bar.

The men were murmuring, urbane, among themselves. Deals were being mulled over, discussed. But the reality was to be there, in the expensive clothes, in the setting like an advertisement. They were talking about a man sitting on the margins of the room. Davros was bending, giving opinions to Stackli and the others.

'They say he's dealing in weapons. He's immensely rich. He's got the white villa by the lake. He's in property too.' The men nodded, approving. 'Weapons are all right. And they usually benefit the right people, where they're exported. I can't see what the fuss is about'. The group was in agreement. 'It's those others who object, who know nothing of business. They're simply envious.' He laughed sarcastically, nodding his head towards those waiting in lines for buses, outside the station opposite the window. 'They live in another way, baby land.'

As she listened to the men Angela could feel Stackli's hand on her leg. She liked it there. Looking across the room she could see the arms business man. She was impressed. Such people maintained her world, had style. Not only did he have money, but he could deal death, make people be killed or not. In an unadmitted part of her she wanted to be able to have such powers. If only she could make herself strong through the money! This was her aim. Without it, she was no-one. Null, at school she had excelled in nothing, had no interests. Only in a fussy way details had mattered to her; the alignment of a cupboard in her parents' kitchen, the precise crease of a skirt, had been all-important concerns, time consuming. Then, when her breasts began to grow she realised she could be sexual, gain access to the world in which details were all.

She knew these men could give her a flat to live in. They'd have the right to visit her. But it would be furnished in the best taste. With their contacts they could get special rates for the best. That would put her one up over the other people, who paid at the full price. She would be saving. This too was one of her passions. It didn't matter which man provided for her. Only Herr Stackli seemed nice. He owned the largest property company in the city too. But a touch of death in a man would be an appeal. Perhaps later she could catch the arms man's eye. Davros was interested too. His arm was resting on the back of her chair, his eyes roved discreetly to her breasts. All was discreet, under ego control, nothing ran free. Everyone could switch themselves on or off, at will. This appealed to her. It was neat, like the smooth running of a sliding kitchen compartment for rubbish bags, in and out without a hitch.

And everyone looked the part. She styled herself on a woman in a chic magazine: her clothes were expensive. The money, of course, meant that she didn't seem like a tart who had shopped in a chain store for a mini-skirt. If her skirts

hanging lights. It would soon be Christmas and the retailers wanted as many customers as possible. Everything had been done with an eye to the cash. The shop windows were full of picturesque women in various clothes and postures. He took her by the arm, masterful, guiding her through the crowds. She wanted to take him and push him face down onto the pavement, kick over the ordinary people who were around her. It came into her head as she walked, how she'd seen on a news programme smart men in khaki suits beating negroes with batons, sending them fleeing. She'd like to be with an upper military man, egg him on to further acts of discipline. But then her ordinary self was coming back, and she was again the elegant woman moving at ease along the pre-Christmas pavements, out for grace and enjoyment.

He drew her up outside a small boutique. The wood round the glass window was deep black, in panels, with golden scrolled lettering. He appreciated the costly job. The pictures stuck behind the glass showed girls in sheeny tights, some with gaps at the tops of the thighs; on others were black body stockings with thongs behind, the breasts bulking large below the thin material. Inside the assistant was all flirty deference; the boxes mounted.

This shop was merely a preliminary. They were heading for an expensive Designer store, where the tightest skirts and dresses were available. He wasn't exactly paying Angela; an outing of this kind had been implicit in their relation from the beginning. It seemed the world of cash pivoted on a queer visual sexuality; selling things went with images of women. In one shop music videos were playing; women lay on the ground while men mimed sex movements over them. Even music couldn't be sold without the girls and their bodies. Women singing by themselves wore brief skirts and moved suggestively. Yet there could be no real touch down the electric system. The shop assistants looked as far as possible like the girls in the music films. Who was real? Who planned it all? The man felt in his element. The money was coming and sexuality was part of its making. Flesh was blank and basic. He would go with anyone behind the curtains of the clothes shops, help the women change. He was insatiable. The images acted on him with a suggestive power.

The girl knew what she was meant to be like. Clinically she assessed the images, gauged which ones she could achieve. She chose shrewdly and he paid. Paying was his power. Day after day he paid for things, and the money that flowed out easily flowed back in. The lights were sharp over their heads as they walked back insulated to the car.

They moved among the other people as if immune from human tasks and conditions. If others were on a lower level, why should they think of them? Yet at times came a glimmer in each, that each was low, a nobody. It pleased him as he passed a bookshop to see the lurid covers on the volumes displayed; the same girls as sold the clothes, music, the rest were on the books too. The world was unified. An awful emptiness that he must have pleasure came to him. They must spend more, eat, see things, not pause. This was the excitement. It came pumping up, as an outpouring to veil the bleak feeling. He had emptied himself and now he must be full.

She saw herself as the exciting woman. She was thinking herself out, as someone who might be read about in a magazine. She had the same enjoyments as the great. Those she saw as the great were exactly those who were featured in her journals or on television as important. Avidly she had run through their life details and tastes down to the sugar bowls on their tables, the President or marketing director or media figure at family breakfast scenes, and copied it all. Copying was second nature.

She had the queer dream in his bed. The men were lined round her in tight uniforms. Behind them lay heaps of bodies, spoilt lives of others left to live. She could corrode the leaders at will, send out an evil force. They were under her control because they all wanted to do things to her. Her sexuality was her weapon, that only worked so long as she was desired. She had to keep them guessing, never be relied upon. Now they would go out and commit crimes on her behalf. The dream faded as she felt the business man reach for her, the globe of his fingers scrabbly under her breast.

It was worth it, to be in this room, with its expensive fittings. Outside lay the city; she was indoors, with a leader. He was moving over her. She wanted to leap into the centre of the room, show herself to him. But now he was waxing sentimental. He'd been drinking and wanted to indulge. He loved his children, he told her. Nothing must harm them. It worried him, the world was dangerous. He would have liked to be an artist.

It would end in itself, coiled up. She would go on with him, in the shops and rooms, acting and reacting, the same sensations, interiors. She felt a safety in the definite repetitions that would come. If he lost interest, she could transfer to another man. Nothing was at stake. There could be no development. Each was static, at the end of a single line. You had sensations, you paid money, you lived in luxury. This was all.

She could hear a choking cry. In the drink he was relaxing, being sentimental. She was sealed up, diamond hard. He was soon back in his suit, genial. The episode wasn't to be referred to. Now he wanted to take a whip to the woman, to people in the street, to himself. He had his place in the city's political organisation, on the right. There were papers to look through later, marketing projects to assess.

Now he held open the box with the bodice in, like the singer had worn on television. He watched the woman stoop to fit herself into it, her breasts hanging. He wanted to run, barge into her, send her rolling on the floor. He reached in a cupboard for a springy rod to lash her with. She liked it, the sudden thrill of the cut, the splash of his urine on her back. Then he was lunging at her, his loins excited, bending like a dog. She was no-one and neither was he.

The doorman opened the heavy door to the hotel respectfully. The man's friends stood and sat at the polished bar, perfectly set out. They were urbane, immaculate. Davros looked across knowingly, a girl beside him. The windows opposite them all, hung round with heavy, expensive curtains, framed the outer life they had made, and risen above. The men represented, they knew, a step on the ladder all out there wished to reach. An air of boredom hung round them. The girl could feel the cuts on her shoulders, liked them there. Herr Stackli had the moist handkerchief in his pocket, where he'd wiped off the arc of her urine from his stomach. He was smart, now, outwardly cool, proud of the cash excess. Through the window they all saw the blocks rising up that they'd had built, the big shops. The city had their features, would repeat itself, sealed in.

The Linguist

The man was rounding the corner. The edge of the supermarket block jutted sharply into the wind. Here it blew especially hard as you turned towards the town. The area was grey and deserted with a few leaves blowing cold against the white tiles of a police station. The man, Simon, was up in thought. Across the road, behind him, was the cemetery where in winter new graves had to be drilled out of the frozen ground. A scheme ran in him, that he was self-righteous, the undervalued one. He glanced aside to the icy graveyard. Outside was a small booth for fried food. Men in anoraks stood around, bleak. He eyed them in appraisal and fear.

He was here, he was safe, he had achieved. A queer exultance raised him up as he passed under the railway that ran by the cemetery. No-one he knew back in England would follow him this far North. He told them all he lived near the Arctic Circle, to put them off. It was true, it was just two hours away by train. He could be isolated, vicious, follow his bents out. And he could pose too as the expert, the man of theory. He smiled the smile he thought was fey and boyish as a young man passed, gave the smirk out.

There were several of them this far North. They'd been recruited by a boss who'd been like them and had wanted to start, as it were, a centre. It had been spoiled, though, this pure male worshipping clique – the boss had retired, others had been recruited. The purity was gone, melted away. The chance had been missed. He was quirky, irritated as he loped down the deserted main street, the neat modern shops each side, opticians, glassware places, small, angular units. He liked the emptiness, the space. For was he not Nordic; he saw himself as the Northern man, white and clean. His blue cord trousers, a relic from years ago, bagged down behind. Perhaps his mother had bought him these. A smug grin was stuck to his face and the snow started a light fall.

They'd be in the bar, he knew, the men like him. He could anticipate the eyes as he went in, the whistling. Some could be bitchy he knew. But he could too, to hold his own. He could keep his head up when the rest were flagging. He'd spent the afternoon at the pool. He liked it, here in the North. The men could sauna together, and then they'd linger, bathing in the shower room, sitting casual on the slab. He'd cast his eyes round, see the naked shapes, the male forms drawing him on. No-one related to him could know – he had carte blanche up here. That was the attraction.

First though was the work. He'd got a class to give at the Institute, helping students pronounce. The road led boringly past blank concrete blocks and a morbid, dark park where bare trees stuck up and dead leaves lay in heaps. He turned past some railings into what resembled a barracks. The smirky grin would be given out to pupils he respected. At meetings he liked to pull faces behind a book held to his face to signal disapproval of speaker's points to favoured acquaintances. He was not to be broached. The hot place at the back of his trousers drove him on to try and twist.

A thin man, chétif, pasty-faced, approached; these men had been in the workplace for twenty years. They knew each other, had the same tastes. As he passed, Simon gave a little mince and skip, to show he was in the know and would go on the trawl later – boys, business men up from Helsinki for a weekend in the health club, he could try them all. But queer noises sounded out in his head, schemes. He would be all powerful. He wanted to show them. The phrases repeated over and over.

Two other men minced along the corridor, both in leather trousers, brown and black. There was a sound of giggles as a door slammed. Then through the door came the drawl of a refined accent 'Oh, but they're such oafs here!' Simon knocked to be let in. The three sat in armchairs like sixth formers at a public school in an old magazine illustration. 'They're not oafs.' Simon glanced round, roguishly. 'They're nice young men.' He held the book up to his face, peeped from behind it, coquetting. 'The new man's ghastly', one of the others started up. 'He's even got a baby.' He emphasised the last word, drawing out the intonation, pulling a face, miming holding a sleeping child, with his lips pouting.

Simon was in the language laboratory, setting the master reels up. The work made no demands but he in his turn exalted it to the heights of importance. Nothing was more crucial than his own course. In this Northern town where he had no contact with anyone who might criticise him he had every incentive to persist in this fancy. As for the Finns, they left him alone. Foreigners were generally risky, and ignored. He'd taught himself Finnish though, and saw himself as the complete Nordic man. He liked privacy and seclusion. No-one liked him and he liked no-one. Sometimes in an irritable mood in which he longed to snap out abuse, some pique after a love night that had gone wrong, he'd drive in his plain small car to a dismal lakeside and sit looking at the water. He longed to scream out abuse, at the lake, at all who weren't like him. He'd drive home in an even worse temper and potter around in his flat. He'd chop up onions on a little board and cook a Northern meal. A boredom ran him through that made him sinister. No-one came to see him. He went nowhere, except to the men's bar, a few drives. Sometimes he went in to work to use the computer on Sundays.

Then, out of the blue, he was elevated to the decision making committee. The regular member was on leave. No-one else wanted to deputise, the meetings were boring and regarded as pointless. His chance had come. Two colleagues were temporary, including the one 'with the baby'. He shivered at the idea of the revolting small creature, perhaps in his flat, damaging his brocaded sofa cover, disordering his computer diskettes. He'd been afraid they'd visit him. One of the men had asked him about contract renewals, how the decision might go. Usually this was a formality. But neither man was pure about Finland. Neither had attended to him, though there'd been no rudeness. He craved maximum endorsements, compliments a virtuoso might receive. Both men liked women, with their ridiculous bosoms and that horrible monthly business that could easily spoil one's flat, he supposed. A surge of resentment came. 'Suppose you'll have us all competing, every three months, with outsiders invited to apply', one man had joked with him. He knew then he wanted it, to make them compete, throw them in jeopardy. His own contract was of course secure. But he'd strike a blow for racial purists and homosexuals, himself, act twisty. How to do it?

The fattish girl, also on the committee, sat in the bar next to him. It was Gays' Evening and she'd come in female capacity. He was outlining to her as the Finns came and went with their cylinders of beer, talking as the alcohol boosted their tongues out of the silence. 'We must put our Department on the map. We must advertise the vacancies every six months.' He heard the noises again and the fat girl slid away, agreeing, to join her dike companion who set drinks on a table. He poked his tongue out at her in jokey gambit, and she rolled hers out back, solid with him. 'I'll support him because I hate those others.' She was giggling with her friend.

Back in his room Simon had got the boy with him who'd been in his class. The boy was small and slight, blond with a dimply simper. He sat in his underpants, listening in to the headphones. The man had been stroking him, leading up to the moment when he hoped he'd power on, exultant to the climax. But now the teenager was uneasy, eyeing him like a captive. Simon had been talking gently, seducing, of the need to compete, to keep people on their mettle, of markets, and millions of applicants for each post, when the boy had spoken up naively: 'Why should people always have to be set against each other?' Quick, flashing, the windy wire of the headphones was three times round the neck of the boy and Simon was pulling, shrieking aloud, 'because I've the power, I say compete, compete.' The boy's hands flailed and Simon loosened the wire. The boy was panting, sitting bowed forward. Simon pushed his chair so he fell. The younger man looked at him from the floor. 'Why you're barmy, that's all. You come here to hide yourself, as no-one can stand you. You're dressed by your mother.' He snatched his clothes, whipped from the room. Simon was pulling the face, the schoolboy sheepish look, caught out and naughty but so winning.

He liked it at work to be friendly, all the students' friend. But sometimes he'd bray out an opinion, say he wanted Finland to be kept pure and undefiled. Some Finns looked at him askance. What was his problem? So most felt. But to a small group he was a rallying point. 'They must come here, learn our language, love our lakes.' The colleague with the child was passing. Simon looked round to his group, conspiring, and with his hand to his mouth whispered 'Not one of us. He doesn't even speak Finnish'. He gave a brief sniggery smirk. But the teacher, whipping round, caught him and Simon wiped the grin away. A hatred ran in him high, though he hung his head in mock penitence.

Back in his flat he liked to dress up in the clothes. He was a Roman orderly who served a famous general. He had black pouchy garments for this. Or there'd be a harness like those used on yachts for hanging out and he'd strap into this to hoist up to swing from a beam. Then he'd be part of an all male, acrobat squad in a German circus, performing to the military. All the time he was meek and mild, outwardly, even humble. He was modest, self effacing, reserved, the true Finn. Yet most Finns were repulsed by him. He'd once explained to a class how he'd stopped all contact with his brother when he realised his brother's accent was improper. The silence that had greeted this communication had been even deeper than usual. He'd seen it as respect. It was true, he'd cut the oaf dead for speaking bad English.

He chopped up the onion in little neat cubes when he got out of the acrobat's harness, and put these in regular lines in a baking dish. He liked everything done 'by the rules'. He would always dress in the same order at the same time when a guest was coming. After he'd put the onions in, there'd be the leather trousers then a white toreador's shirt. He'd sleek his hair back and polish his glasses and feel kingly, intellectual, a sportsman who read Gide. In his fantasy no-one could down him. But bubbling below was the undermining surge that he was no-one. He never consciously recalled how he'd wired up the boy. He was gracious, elegant to himself.

The bell rang and he loped over to let the guests in. A short man in dark glasses eased into an armchair; an arrogant, thin man sat in another, his leather trousers tight, pointy shoes crossed. Simon did the smirk and put on music.

'Oooh, I love the thirties.' He was camping, doing the gestures. The guests raised eyebrows, to endorse, squeezing hands as Simon got drinks. The short man eyed the room, spoke in a low voice. 'Can't stay more than an hour. I've got a date with the play group man.' He disliked his host. The others ignored him. The meal was eaten swiftly, then they were up, out in the snow, walking together on the pavement in long coats heading for the bar.

The men were dancing, putting on a camp chant, showing solidarity. On a video screen a scroll of men's photographs and their addresses was showing. A few dancers were bare chested with little braces over. The man with the pointy shoes was eyeing up Simon. 'How's that committee? Got the heteros out yet?' Simon gave the downward wave of his hand. 'It's hard – but Lyn's on our side'. They all knew Lyn: everyone knew everyone of the same bent. 'With her it will be two to one, voting. We'll win.' The two men put their arms up in the clenched fist and did a little dance. There was a synthesiser band playing now, and the screen showed a London swimming pool, men in the changing rooms.

There'd been many such evenings. On the walk home Simon had been pulling the faces, muttering abuse. He was tired. He'd been in a side room, done some driving, but wasn't satisfied. Some evil was baying in him, a loose desire for harm. He looked round his living room, eyed the neat fittings, let out the shriek against himself. He would howl like a dog in his closet, pull distorted faces in the mirror, then look at his reflection with a military cap on, the officer manly and up to his duty.

'You see, they don't know Finnish. The other candidates do.' He sat in the office of the boss, thin legs in old blue corduroy stretched out, feet in brown socks and old sandals. The fat girl was nodding, in support. The boss was fed up with these people, but outnumbered. 'So you vote them out, in spite of their work?'

'Yes, we vote them out.' Simon was triumphant. He skipped to his office at the end of the session; his man friend was inside. They were giggling, up in arms. Simon believed he'd done right. He'd acted on behalf of Finland itself, defended it. The two temporary men would have to leave. He felt himself heat with desire. He'd give in, in his own office, melt out white there and then. He gave a sigh of surrender.

It was cold out in the street, hard to breathe the air. You slid as you walked on the ice that had formed on the snow surface. He was watching the ground. He threaded the town, the shops lit up at night. The cry was forming in his brain, to exult. He longed to wipe himself across the world, be the non-pareil. The subway below the railway was deserted. He came up the ramp and there were the men by the food booth. Suddenly two were there at his side, 'Going my way?' These Finns were big like shot putters, snickering, in anoraks. Then he was against the wall. 'What about Petri?' The bigger of the pair pressed him with his stomach. Simon was writhing, half liking the feel of the big man, half afraid. 'I don't know him.'

'You do. You half strangled him in your flat. You're sick.' The other Finn was eyeing the Englishman in contempt. 'Let's leave him. He's U.K. trash.' The shot putter eased him from the wall, threw him on, up the slope.

As he walked, Simon knew the smirky feelings were coming back. He'd got away with it. He pulled the face as he crossed to the wall adjacent to the cemetery. There was a barrier across the path. He'd have to make a detour on the pavement that ran just inside the wall, on the edge of the graveyard. A few lights flickered. Then he felt a hand round his neck. It was the temporary men. He was in the pit of a newly blasted grave. He made the waaing cry. He could see the legs of the temporary men above him, firm in the vague light. One of them had thrown off his fur coat and was dancing in bathing trunks on the grave's edge. 'To give you a good send off, this final pleasure.' Again Simon felt the smile, like on a boy caught out at school, creep to his face. He wanted to prostrate himself, then have revenge. The man put his coat back on, spoke. 'You've got a thick coat on. We're going to tether you up like a goat.' Simon let off the braying noise. 'Free competition, meant no harm, only thinking of the best interests, no hard feelings.' The temporary men were silent. They put on little masks with goat noses and whiskers and began to dance. Then they roped him round the shoulders and tied the ends to sticks hammered into the icy ground. His ordeal lasted five minutes. Then he was set free. 'We're leaving tomorrow. Then you can be race-pure, male-pure again.' The temporary men faded into the dark.

He gave the howl back in his flat, looked round at the

wooden unit with his tapes on in alphabetical array. He'd cry on a man's lap, be soothed with his head on another's worsted knee. He'd seen a film once where this had happened. There'd been a fire blazing, a quadrangle outside, male voices sporting. The phrase became a fixation, 'worsted knee'. He whispered it till he had to scream it out, 'worsted knee.' He wanted mad things, a line of choir boys in surplices to serve him cakes, someone to climb up his fire escape and rape him in his room. But no, he would console himself with linguistic studies. He set the book out, switched the VDU on. Then he was spinning and kicking, his computer diskettes whirling about him like a catherine wheel, he was calling out 'worsted knee'. Petri should soothe him. He lifted the phone and longed for the youth to stroke his hair. Then he'd turn and power the boy into the ground, like the pictures in his magazine.

At the School

The road was cold and black, shining in the early morning light with the wet. A few cars passed, that was all. Bits of rubbish lay outside the high, queer entrance to the flats, built like walls, with tall oblong entrance sections like those to grim castles. The inhabitants didn't make this comparison. Only someone from outside might see things in this way.

There was nothing in the street to relieve the black. Rather, all acted as reinforcement. A cold, strong wind blew and a drizzle hung in the unclean air. People had begun to pass along the pavements to work. Only the new modern office blocks added a cleanness, hard, and a domination to the landscape.

The bus came in, meaningless. To ride the distance each day, participate in the act of wage labour, was this the modern fulfilment? The human lives sat on the seats, to be ferried to their respective work confines. All was reduced, shut back to a low level of poverty of several kinds.

A little group of school children stood near the roundabout, at the terminus. Rubbish was scattered over the dirty walkways. There were a newsagent's, run by an Indian family, take away chip cafés and an old toilet below road level. Big lorries with trailers passed. The air itself was heavy with a weight of chemical waste. The school children were waiting to jeer, to throw stones, bottles, at anyone they disliked.

Over the whole area was an implication of violence. Each day incidents occurred. A girl, walking home in the evening, would be clubbed on the head. Shops would be held up by men with knives and guns. A cyclist, knocked down by a car, would then be stabbed by the driver. Everyone was used to the catalogue. What else could be expected? A diseased resignation rose up out of the dirt of the street, spread out into the lives of those living there. All was down, the bad spirit taking you back to nowhere, not enough money, not enough anything.

The walk to his workplace lay along the main road, between the high blocks of flats. They stood in a high, long line, angular, part of the council estate that extended for fifteen miles round about. Nothing relieved the hard, low landscape. The buses and lorries moved, beneath the grey sky, with the blocks on each side. Yet here actual people were expected to live their lives out. The power of adaptation gripped them; all should adapt, be low, to survive here. A crude, logical life view prevailed, in which orthodoxies of brutality, fitting in, were dominant.

The ugly gates of the yard were set open in the area adjoining the flats. A stream of school children passed in, then pupils loitered about the glass entrance doors. It was a shabby place, run down and sick looking. As he passed a crowd of youths a chant went up, like a muttering of frustrated beasts: 'Punishments, punishments!' The boys would egg him on, to punish them. A curious, brutal atmosphere prevailed. Political organisations of the extreme Right drew support from such areas.

He pushed on in through the doors, hating the contact. His back was tense with resistance, the need also not to show you were affected. He knew the pupils would enjoy to see a sign of discomfort, on his part. Inside the entrance stood a man in a black funereal suit, shouting instructions: 'Take care sonny! Go back, sonny, and come in again.' It was all unreal. The children wriggled and smirked, wanting to see how much they could get away with. A great impulse to insult and do harm was in them, if they could.

The man moved in a dream up the stairs, not awake. It was an accident, he reflected, to be there at all. There was no meaning in it for him, or most of the pupils, save friction and dislike. Other work possibilities had not existed, at the time he had begun. A disillusion in him had resulted in such employment. Why should he care what happened to him? Now, after a few months in this new place, the need to care about his own activity was evident. He was brought down, reduced to a lowness. In part he had wanted this.

Up in his class he took the register. Boys of sixteen sat jeeringly at desks. Several wore pullovers with the name of a luxury designer on them. Many were already proud of a reputation for theft or violence. A small minority were sensitive. Only there was no chance for the sensitive to affect the overall ethos.

It was pointless. Lesson followed lesson. Sometimes, in one or two pupils, came a glimmer of interest. Otherwise the whole institution was wrong. What was the point for them all to be there, in that way, when most of them would be better off elsewhere, engaging in quite other activities? He overheard through the uproar of his own class the teacher next door shouting and bullying her children to get on with some writing about a poem. Some were shouting abuse back at her. Outside he saw the flats, ever present and sharp edged, the crowded road curving through the heavy estate. Beyond was a dismal park where no-one went in case they were attacked. The pupils sat on in the class, reluctant to read, write, do anything. Why should he force them?

The children saw a young man, an object, before them. Why didn't he slap them about, be punitive, drill them? They couldn't understand the apathy that engrossed him. So they messed about, watching for the punishment. What they liked best was to be divided into groups and left to gossip, ostensibly about a poem, if it was English, but in fact about themselves. They were simple. It was best for them to have a simple teacher who would slap them about, help them to pass menial exams so they could go out and be social menials. Preferably this teacher should be only slightly less lazy than they were, and without any cultural aspiration beyond their own.

Any other kind of teacher they would proceed to cut down. A few of the teachers kept up a hypocrisy of higher aims, but in the end all the education led up to was the preparation for menial exams and jobs. In fact the pupils would benefit from a quite different kind of school. But here the nasty pretence of 'helping', with the overshadowing objective of exam passing for jobs, was the rule. The pupils were to be flattered and bullied into enough knowledge to pass simple exams. Over all loomed the flats, the angular, ugly outer world.

These were the forgotten people. The poor stay poor in most cases, the menial give birth to those who stay menial. Such people have the worst; the worst housing, doctors, schools, shops, everything bad. A whole culture of low, reduced scrabbling prevails in such areas, where most of the adult individual energy goes in financial scraping, working for those others who live elsewhere, in quite other circumstances. Even if they passed their simple exams the pupils would stay down, in the lowest positions. This they knew, and it fed their antagonism.

In the staff room he sat silent at his table, after the classes, switching out connection. The day passed like a narcotic. It was true, you forgot most things as you moved in the ugly classrooms, suspended in the brutal vale, always waiting for the next jeer, keeping the violence at bay. You felt like an object, unclean, your flesh turned to ugly will. He task was hard, the pay low, confirming that most held this duty in low esteem. Who would work here for three pounds an hour? Yet most of the teachers were doing that. The very pupils despised them.

At the end of the day the teachers left speedily, pleased to be gone. Most felt trapped there, locked down in a world they felt they could not leave. They had to put up with it. They were passive, accepting the orthodox creed. They were jeered at from all sides.

He waited again at the bus stop, to return. A heavy rain

fell now in the dusk, trapping down the exhaust fumes, making the air ponderous to breathe. The roof of the shelter jutted out, sharp below the rain. Everywhere you looked were hard, sharp edges. A huge pub was adjacent, with garish advertisements for pool and snooker, various drinks, topless nights. Ragged groups of school pupils passed, incoherent, the jeer always ready. The lorries swung towards him, off the roundabout. It was a total enclosure of poverty and ugliness, deprivation. The mainstays of life outside work here were drinking, the television and a lurid sensationalism which issued, in its extreme form, in rapes, violent robbery. Nothing flourished here. On the other hand, since the implication of foul living was too disturbing to grasp, the refuges of escape were partly understandable. To know anything in this place was to be tortured by awarenesses that all was ugly and unfair. When the outer world is unrewarding, fantasy is the escape.

This was the human world, these were human people! The estate stretched on and on as the bus moved on, houses small on each side of the road in ugly sameness. Dirty playing fields every two miles – relics from some past time of hopeless civic concern – relieved the brick. But no-one ventured into these. The grass was dark and unhealthy, the risk of attack was great.

He got off on a little rise in the middle of a development of shops. It was all appalling and foul. Groups of unemployed men hung about the shopping precinct, looking wicked or hopeless, eyeing the girls, or else staring into space. They had nothing. For them the world was a succession of centres: the town centre, the shopping centre, the job centre, the benefit centre. Life was brought down to this level. The people moved on the pavements in their normal world, passed the offers in the windows urging them to buy. Some shopkeepers acknowledged the poverty by advertising in their windows that DHSS claimants were welcome. Grants could be obtained – rarely – for the cheapest of basic furniture, carpets. Further on the chimney of the car factory sent out smoke and chemicals. The landscape was in a state of attrition.

The next day the procedure would be the same. He would rise in the small cramped room in the council house and get ready for work. This room he rented, all he could afford, from an old couple. There was no cooker in the room, nor was one permitted, so all food had to be cold. Outside a freezing fog lay across the street, glistening with dirty moisture. Like a subject in a trance, tomorrow he would take the ride to the workplace. The classes would be in wait for him, the pupils alert for anything peculiar to attack and drive out. The abuse would start at the gates. Other teachers drove in, if they could afford a car, afraid of what might be said to them if they approached on foot. Their cowering was additional fuel for the pupils' contempt. Poor themselves, the pupils despised poverty.

Inside a bell rang. The lessons would commence. He pushed again through the mass of smirking pupils at the main door, entered the staff room. His spirits sank at the prospect of the day, so uninspired. To be in this place, to be derided in any efforts to aid – he was no Christian, to be nailed up in this paltry task.

As the man moved towards the stairs, the class were already up in the high room, and against him. He climbed the dirty stairway wearily; a white tiled floor was broken and muddy beneath his feet. There was no time to look out of the window, to live. In any case there was nothing to see out there, just a black park, a small lake concreted round its edges, rubbish projecting from its surface, then the road and the endless flats. The day would pass like an opiate, but without vision or thought. Only the mechanical task of the teaching remained. You had to be always on the watch, waiting for the jeer, the descent into the obscene or violent.

It was tedious, this work. The door swung open and there were the faces, waiting. In a different setting he might have liked some of the faces, but here, in this place, feeling was suspended. He noticed without a qualm the familiar obscene abuse chalked on the blackboard, the class alert, gloating, to watch his reaction. He ignored the writing. Even outside there would be perversions and twists in these people. Groups of pupils had taken to setting fire to houses in the area, turning on the gas taps and fleeing, in hope of an explosion. These groups were a minority, but an extreme statement of the general mood.

The lesson was to be on a book he liked a lot. The class began to read aloud. A fat boy was dragging the words out, deliberately making the text ugly and tedious. This was one of the 'exam books'. Plainly the class as a whole had no interest in it, except as an object to sneer at, or deride. Perhaps two pupils wished to read it properly.

It was a game. A slow, broad boy, leering, put up his hand. 'Why can't we do the bit about the rape? I saw the film. There's a rape in it!' A boy at the back was calling out, 'I seen it on the video; – the rape!' The other boys were smiling, the girls giggling. The text itself was a bore to them, extraneous to their lives, context, minds. The exam decreed they should be here in this room, reading it. Otherwise they had no interest in it. The exam once passed, if it was passed, all awareness of the book would drop out of them. Many would never read such a book in their lives again. This was legitimate. In a way he pitied them all, the teacher, to be placed in the false position they were in. Only he hated them for sneering. 'Why don't you teach us then, Sir?' 'Yeah, why don't you? Rape, rape, rape! This is boring!' The voices chimed in together.

It was curious how he forgot himself at these times, ceased to exist just there, passed out into the dirty landscape beyond the glass of the windows, to escape. The faces were in front of him but he had no connexion with them. Sometimes he would engage the pupils in abuse, send them out or to be disciplined. But the Senior Teachers, officially responsible for such discipline, disliked being bothered, made it clear that it was a weakness in himself, in their eyes, to send pupils out.

The class grew noisier and noisier. The pupils liked to goad him with words, cry out insults. Poetry was another mistake with this group: 'It's boring, it don't mean nothing.' Even patient explanation drew this response. The girls liked to sit designing hearts with their boyfriends' names on, or else sit gossiping with each other, turning from this to join in the attack on the master.

After such lessons he would descend the dirty stairs again, left filthy because of economies in cleaning. Once, at the top, a pupil from an adjoining classroom gave him a push, short, vicious. Another teacher had fallen a few weeks back and broken a foot. He too had been pushed, but had refused to admit it, nervous of losing face in front of his colleagues. Sometimes teachers were assaulted by groups of youths. Such men left the school, not to be mentioned. There was a reluctance to confront the full violence in some of the pupils, consciously to acknowledge their hatred and derision. So teachers would keep secret the disorder in their classes, the insults they received daily.

A knot of boys approached along the lower corridor where dust hung, lit up by the winter light. He could hear the muttering begin, 'Wanker! Wanker! Wanker!' hear the low chant, see the grins on those who heard. The grins switched to sneers, then insolent innocence, quickly affected if he glanced in their direction. The long dirty corridor stretched out, its drab yellow walls containing them all in ugliness. A murderous spirit rose in him, to fall on the pupils in violence. But, ultimately, he was profoundly more indifferent. Later, if he was in the mood, he'd take trouble to discipline them. Now, tired, he couldn't be bothered.

The day drifted on, in a remoteness that was a drug of oblivion. Lesson followed lesson. The brain grew tired, the body too, but the need to fight for order persisted. Sometimes there was more or less peace. But over all came the sense that it was futile. Why bother here, with this? What was being achieved, in the friction?

The staff room jutted out at the side of the ugly main building. From its windows, like a control tower, you could see the flats arranged in grim towers across a scrappy patch of swampy green. The pupils were hurrying out, as if from a place of dread or derision. Sometimes a fight broke out in the road and a crowd would gather. The fights were vicious. In the evening they might be continued with stabbings, or robberies, down subways and alleys, the destructive impulse finding outlet that way. The whole area was sealed in poverty and reduced aspirations. As he stared out of the window a van ran past in the rain, polythene covering its load of electronic games machines, popular entertainments in this zone.

He sat down tired, at the table, with the rest. All were despondent. The day had been a failure for all of them. A few knew, others kept up a bluster of confidence. But most sensed that conditions were in some way out of control, the violence building up.

Through the windows loomed the flats, the wide road curving with its weight of cars across the dirty grass, the council estate stretching on for miles: out there the violence also had its origin. The people could not get out of the total immersion in the zone. They sealed themselves further in as a refuge, using the electronic games, television and video programmes, drink, as the material for the fantastic evasion they required. Who could identify and know the real situation? To think of it was to enter a disturbed world of lost meanings, betrayals, injustice. Yet, lacking conscious knowledge, even the simplest of the pupils had an inkling that all here had been given a bad chance, to be born here, in such an area. It was arbitrary, who was placed where. There could be no doubt, though, that to grow up in such a place was to be severely restricted. It was no good making the poor life romantic. The local paper recorded the mean crimes, petty stabbings, break-ins, spiteful rapes and assaults the environment fostered.

Outside the exposed path led brutally past the flats. A crowd of loitering pupils sent up a jeery chant as he passed, 'Fuck you, fuck you, fuck you!' The day was over. Tomorrow all the teachers would be there again, and so it would go on. You could lose yourself in the cycle of numbing repetition, turn your power of freedom to ashes, in such places, limit your possibilities to the low level that prevailed. All this could be done under the cloak of care or help. It wasn't true, though, that you could substantially raise the level of views or feelings that prevailed. Rather you were drawn down too, at the lowest level, forced into contact with the abuse, and the madly bitter, narrow views. You were fighting also the social force that had created these ugly people and the area, aware all the time that the same babies, placed more fortunately, could have quite other lives.

As he walked in the dusk he heard the crash of an empty bottle hit the road behind him. The glass scattered hard in the cold air across the filthy pavement. A few passers-by turned nervously, walked hurriedly on. He saw two boys run down one of the sideroads lined with council houses. As a rule the teachers were afraid to walk alone in such an area, so close to the school, either driving in and out, as it were, in the closed security of their cars, or else walking in a group of three or four together, and only in daylight. He was too new to realise the unstated principle. The bottle hadn't been meant to hit him, just constitute a warning. He wondered what he was to these people, that they could want to do such things.

At the dark bus stop a few poor people waited. Old, dirty men, ragged children in thin coats that wouldn't protect them much from the January cold, stood in the wet. The traffic poured from the roundabout, sending out heavy exhaust vapours into the air, already thick and leaden to breathe. No-one protested here. An unconscious stoicism dominated. On the surface there was sometimes cheerfulness. But the people here were down, and they knew it. They had to fight for all they got. There were no special privileges or advantages here. This was the reverse side of such things.

The bus was warm, a relief from the stop. It ran on into another suburb. Upstairs were the shouts and bangs of the pupils. Other passengers tried to ignore them, uneasy, or else attempted to find the disruption a joke. All was squalid, mean, round about, with a tang of disease in the air, coughing, weary movement. Any beauty or brightness was here up against the ugliness that prevailed wherever you looked. A sensitive form would die off soon, under weight of the drab, enclosing seal.

Tomorrow it would begin again, the job. There would be no way to continue for much longer here. He sat in a poor café, before taking the train through the vast estate, a few stops along the line. The people round him were ragged, done down. An old lady was shaking at a nearby table, ugly and dirty. The waitress came across. 'What's the matter, love?' She felt the old woman's hands, head, realised the woman was freezing, shaky and weak. She rubbed her with her own hands, trying to restore warmth. He heard the ambulance coming, as he turned into the station. What could be done, to wipe out the poverty? The injustices were heavy and many. He remembered the jeering of the pupils, the nasty chanting of the louts and his own sympathy went dead for the time. Whatever the cause, the fact of the vileness was real, to be loathed.

The train ran on, into the wet, muddy night. The housing estate spread out on each side of the tracks, with the coloured lights of the television screens already burning out fantasy in most of the homes as the train passed.

The street outside the station was black and dark. Lines of people queued along the road for buses. He turned to walk down the main street. Take away food bars lined the road, shops with electrical goods, videos and video hire centres. The passive were well pandered to here. High blocks rose up behind the shops, for housing, offices. The road grew darker, menacing, with older, dismal flats with caged in balconies down one side. The grass in front of these shone black in the dim street lighting, scattered with empty crisp packets, bottles, tatters of paper. There was an older Victorian warehouse converted to a Sikh temple at the end of his road. An old, white bearded Indian man passed slowly, the eyes rolling, in a state of distraction, dazed and lost.

The council houses began again. In one of these was the upper room, his home. In this lair, in the centre of the ugliness, an escape could be plotted.

The next day the teaching went on, like before. For hour after hour he stood or sat in classrooms. It was nearly the last class of the afternoon. A smallish youth, like a wiry old man shrunk with age and with the pointed features of a rat's face, was banging on the desk, singing, casting all the time challenging looks at the teacher. At intervals he would beat his forehead hard on the desk. Round him his friends kept up a supportive bang. In a low voice he was muttering, 'Cut you up, Cut you up. I hate you, I hate you. Cut you up!'

The boy wriggled in his seat. His small, cringing buttocks squirmed in the tight beige trousers, cheap and ugly. The rat boy wanted to resist, to jeer at everything, to fill the world with his own hatred. The rest of the class were watching, hoping for excitement. 'Get out!' The boy made no movement. 'Make me.' Another older teacher was passing. The boy subsided, became docile all at once. Then, when the other teacher was gone, a string of abuse tore out of him. 'Fuck! Fuck! Fuck! I hate you!' The wizened boy beat his head on the desk lid, like a psychopath. Other boys joined in, singing loudly an obscene song. The girls sat watching, pleased. 'We'll rip you up. We'll rip you up!' the chant began.

The teacher was bored, disgusted. Even if this were a

show, it was still a sick display. He knew it was not a show. Such boys, youths, plenty like these, would roam the streets of the suburb at night, stabbing those perceived as enemies, rivals, intruders, stealing money, cars, like urban rats. They were so far gone in hate, they could not be brought back into any other mode, except by a stronger will. Even then the return would be a temporary pretence. They lived in hate. The teacher could not waste his own energy, worn out as it was by the constant, mechanical teaching, in dominating these pupils. Why should he try to become their will?

Some were young members of the National Front, would go out cutting up the faces of foreigners in their area. All might respond to the command of some officer in the army, to brutal orders and punishments. They liked these, just as they liked themselves to bully and dominate, like dictators. When they did get up enough energy to write in class they might choose a sadistic theme, how they were part of a white mercenary army sent out to kill the black people and torture them in Africa. Or else they might fantasise to be gangleaders. Partly they would do this to annoy teachers they saw as 'progressive', but largely they expressed what they really liked. The misspelt, pathological sentences, like psychopath's utterance, were written out in a dirty scrawl. Lacking the energy to complete even these, the pupils would tail off after two feeble paragraphs, and sit for the rest of the lesson in aggressive silence, or else make violent mutterings, 'Rip, rip, rip', or talk loudly about rapes they'd seen on their family video. They liked to fart and belch, degrade themselves. In the area around the school there were many actual rapes.

In such circumstances the teacher was nauseated. Why should time be wasted on such people? He wasn't a police official, an army officer, a sadist, or a psychiatrist, yet to deal with these types he had to become all of these. He would be paid for this about one hundred pounds a week. The pupils were against him, had shown their derision. He went to fetch a Senior Teacher, to remove the boy who had refused to quit the class. The boy was wild, struggling and abusing: 'I hate you for this, I hate you all.' At last the door closed on him. The other pupils were insolent, recalcitrant, throwing paper around, singing in defiance.

After the class the chief of his section of work approached. It was clear she blamed him for the trouble. 'It's how you treat them – that's why they jeer. You have to please them, be encouraging. Don't ask them to write.' 'Why should I please people like that?' He remembered their abuse. The answer irritated the woman. She didn't reply, and walked away. The pupils were watching, ready to chant out 'Punishments, punishments!' as he walked by. In truth he hated and despised the fact of them whatever the cause of their sickness might be. For, even if there were explanations of deprivation, this didn't alter the fact that to him such pupils were humanly vile. Their mean crimes and attitudes, the rattling jeer that rose spontaneously in their thin throats so often – these were features to be loathed.

The day ended in a queer bitterness. A sharp wind blew hard round the edge of the flats, over the dirty iced-up craters of water, set into the lawns. The darkness settled down, like a weight across the vacant landscape. He felt his lungs working against a pressure. The air felt also dirty and corrupt in his mouth and nostrils.

He didn't want to stay there, use his life up in that way. Even if some worthwhile work could be done, it would be of so small a measure that the energy used in completing it would be disproportionate. He didn't have the missionary zeal for self-sacrifice required. Besides, it was obscene to offer oneself up on this altar, or any. To work oneself out, for what?

He remembered the bottle smashing behind him, the groups of jeerers, the chants. He didn't love these people. A hate rose up in him for many of them, how they wanted to trample down effort or delicacy. In his imagination he reviewed the faces of the pupils. There were a few he liked. The rest were a mass who could not benefit from attending such a place. It was a cruelty to force it on them. They required different treatment.

Suddenly, nearing the bus stop, he was conscious of a crowd of youths closing round him, as he crossed a stretch of waste ground. He saw the sneering face of a fat boy, with short cropped hair like a private in the army. He knew they wouldn't dare a physical attack in daylight. He walked on. A myth had started up among the simpler pupils that he was a homosexual. He shared a flat with a teacher at the school who was one. That he taught poetry had added fuel to this fancy. 'Been sucking cocks, Sir?' Another boy cut in. 'I'd like to come round your house tonight, and fuck you right up your bum, Sir.' The master passed on his way, and the boys melted back into the doorways of the flats as the busier street grew nearer. He ignored the insults until the next day when he would discipline those responsible. These were people to flatter, and encourage.

The flats loomed up, all round in the wind. The suburb stretched for miles, in all directions, like its own land, with its own laws and assumptions. There were many such areas in the English cities. A well of malice and hate was set there, in the centre of the deprivation. The landscape itself was vile and ugly; lines of houses stretched out, small dirty and unrelieved, little shops where big roads crossed, video hire centres. What was needed here? The people were sealed in, proud of their own blankness, many vicious and foul, ready to stab and revile, ridicule. Anyone who seemed different or foreign was to be attacked. The policy worked; few immigrants came to live here, among the workers.

The flats were all around. He would leave the place before his own power to respect or respond went dead and atrophied.

The Queer Man

The common stretched out, the wiry turf in the sun's glare green and gleaming. A few businessmen were walking their dogs; in the distance stood their houses with the mock timbers, the bogus connection with the past. Ask them, and they knew nothing of this tradition their houses aped. Watching from behind the bushes was the queer man, who they didn't know about either.

The grass stretched towards the scrubby edges of the common where the wind blew the bushes into waves. The man was out alone, hanging around. He'd come from the council estate a few miles off. He could see the rich people's houses on the edge of the green. The timbered walls shone in the sun. The period touches were reminiscences. He didn't know any history. A queer feeling was in him today, that nothing could happen for him anymore. There was no job, and he'd not be likely to get one. He was down, by himself. The bushes seemed to laugh at him as he stood there, the branches twitching in the wind, somewhere else. He remembered the chink of a red spade on a tin bucket on a seaside holiday he'd had as a boy. Now nothing had come of it.

He watched the business man go past with a dog. He was still in his suit, the man, and the dog was whitish, plump and rather old. The urge came, as he watched, that he would run up and plunge the knife in the walker's back, then be gone. No-one would see him. Instead he stepped out from the bush and gave a grimace at the startled walker. All around the two men the empty grassland flickered below the clouds that blocked and unblocked the sunshine. The grimace given he ran off, jumping in the air and twinkling his legs like a leaping sheep. There was the hint of a ballet side kick in the movement.

'Awfully queer, darling.' The businessman sat at his oval oak table with the silver knives out. His wife looked across at him, sceptical. She didn't like her husband. Through the window she could see the grass waving, the neat trees on the lawn, the remoter suburbs and knew behind these the houses of the poor.

'A queer man lurking on the common. He seemed to pull a face and run off.'

'What kind of face?' The husband twisted his features into a mouth open gape, and a neck posed slightly to one side.

'And he jumped up, too, as if in derision.'

'What of?'

'Who knows?' They looked round the room, complacent. There was nothing to deride.

He'd wanted to stab the business man, set the blood running. All was over for himself so why not for others too? Also there was a certain zest in the idea, a social revenge. If life was meaningless – and his own was – then what did it matter? They should all rise up. He could imagine the common set out lurid with a hundred men in suits lying horizontal. But no-one else would rise up. He was the isolated saviour, spoken to by God. A kind of blahhing sound echoed under his skull, probably God speaking, he reflected, a whir of phrases crossing him. He was no-one but a criss-cross of this and that, meanings merging into slime. They gave him a weekly grant and he had to sign for it, he could live in a slum room where he kept the food on the window sill upstairs and had no cooker. He could see the colourful packs, damp at the base, the jolly ladies printed in the picture. Queer thoughts came of revenge and attack. In a vague way he held the women responsible. The daily sight of them on the packets confirmed this impression.

To make it all derelict and dirty, where the nice houses were, to give the women a shock, this was the aim. So he'd stand, menacing, in his mac and ludicrous trousers with bells sewn on like a morris dancer, mostly hidden by bushes to alarm women out walking. Or else he'd wear a sequinned shirt and black tight trousers like an ice dancer whose fortunes he'd followed regularly on television. He'd tried it once, out on the moorland in skates, but had found it hard going, the blades caching in the turf and cramping his gigolo turns and glides. So far it had all been a joke, he'd felt, like laughing at philosophy, pulling faces at people to make them start, or alarming them by walking or running oddly. English people were easily startled, he felt; the smallest oddity and they'd shy away. They'd be easy to murder, they were so scared of everything. He could feel the jeer against himself rise up, the widespread condemning of his stance.

Yet he had another life, quite separate, in which he owned a better flat in a smart area. He could be urbane, talking the way people liked to hear it, smart and discussing investment opportunity. This self was as real as the other. He sat behind an antique desk with leather top-work and even wore spectacles, looking alert and wily. It was only when the bad blood beat up he had to switch, to come and go to the council house room. For half of the week he was there, throwing food at the walls and watching videos. The skater would turn, leg outstretched, partnering the girl, heaving her over his shoulder in her ornate costume. He liked it when one fell, made a mistake. He'd rerun the sequence then. He liked to see scenes of humiliation. He'd go out in his poor man's costume, and then dress up in public toilets – a convenient place to change – to proceed to the Conservative Club. There he was a respected member, consulted on financial issues. He knew the rhetoric, how to take a hard line. Then he'd be back in his cheap room, smearing the salad cream on the chairs and singing as he did so, sitting on packs of bought chips in his underpants, wriggling and rearing. He could be whatever he wanted. He would be an Eighteenth Century farmer taking the hounds to the New Age Travellers, beating them with Neptune's trident as they handed in their giros at the Post Office, whipping them back to their cavalcade of decrepit vehicles. They were 'something for nothing' people. He'd encircle them at Stonehenge with Rotweilers, snap them down.

Once he'd started a study course and a certain passage had caught his fancy. He'd given up the course later, and in fact already had a degree from Oxford. He liked theory, anything lucid. The passage ran: 'the concepts, apparently unchanged in themselves, will be subject to a mutation of meaning or rather will be struck by the loss of sense towards which they slide, ruining themselves immeasurably.' The meaningless text impressed him; he saw it as la clarté, not obscure. It gratified him, to connect himself with such apparent thought. He would be their representative, the shifting concepts, moving on towards nihilism and murder. He'd torn out the page from the book and kept it stuffed in a Marmite pot on the radiator.

It was odd how people seemed to like him. When he was up, in his suit, with his case, on the train to London – for he sometimes rode from the sedate country town to the Stock Exchange – everyone was courteous, the ticket collector obsequious even, and he looked the success. Yet clad up in his mac and morris dancer's trousers he was beyond the margin, a man en route to perversion. Now and then he'd splash himself with the salad cream for extra effect. Once he forgot himself and turned up in the pervert's outfit at the Conservative Club and was rudely turned away, unrecognised, even though he'd spoken at the door in praise of tough monetary policy and claimed the poor would be always a social fact. Somehow on this occasion he'd got confused between his two identities and seemed to inhabit neither. He'd tried a quote from a political thinker's book – left or right it was all the same now – about how anyone who wanted to buy a scholarly paperback book, or a mansion on Lake Como, would, of course, put themselves in a position to buy one, motivation being all, but even this hadn't got him entry. After changing in a nearby toilet into his stockbroker's outfit he was admitted not much later, with deference; 'we had a pervert trying to get in, guv' the doorman had confided.

Now it was more ominous. He was waiting with the knife behind the bush. He had on the outfit, with the addition of a jester's hat and bars of chocolate fixed to strings dangling from a belt round his waist. No-one had come by, but he could now see in the distance the figure of a woman approaching. He recognised her as the wife of one of his clients. She drew nearer across the scrappy grassland, her curly dog trotting low-slung and plump nearby. In the distance a man rode a scrambler motorbike down a cinder path and disappeared. Nearer she came until she was within two feet: he sprung out and stood blocking her path with his jester's stick to the fore; he did the queer dance to make his bells jingle, jumping to scissor his legs, quite graceful. She gave a light scream and then smiled:

'Why, Mr Jackson. I hardly recognised you. You're on your way to the pageant.' He gave a roar to make the bells tinkle and bars shake. He wanted to define himself, swerve like an ice dancer. The knife was warm in his hand but he kept it hidden yet. He tried a few tap steps, speaking to the rhythm.

'How's your Peps bond doing? You had Tessas too?'

'Sweet of you to remember. Isas also. Fine yield so far.' She had a soft spot for the stockbroker.

The knife struck her hard and Jackson was in his element, plunging and swaying like a Ninja warrior he'd seen on video. He wanted to send the knife spinning to harvest the tree tops and then be chased by devil monks. The atrocity was like one out in Malaysia he'd read about. A colonialist had stabbed down a native maid for insubordination. Women were like natives, risky and suspicious. Their pictures were on his food boxes. He gave more lunges. Leonard Woolf had beaten the pearl fishers aside with a light heart. The clouds were moving across the sun and the woman lay still on the dark grass. The jester's rod was next to her and he danced the tinkly dance. She'd been no-one and he was no-one. He sat down to get his breath back. The knife hadn't spun back from the bush he'd thrown it into. He was vaguely disappointed it wasn't all more like the film. In the distance a two car diesel unit hooted. He didn't like vulgar things. He would change in the toilet near the club.

The next day he was at the desk, exhilarated, fresh with the financial advice. He was spruce and clean, a white Afrikaaner. Although his dancer's outfit hung in his office cupboard he had no recollection of having been on the moor.

The Foreign Wife

She had flown in earlier that week, from Mexico City. Back home were her three children, her husband. She looked forward each year to this summer trip. In the year she acted the part of the dutiful wife. But she was beset with tensions, odd symptoms. Her body ached, she was tired all the time. There was something missing.

She had married the rich lawyer when she was young, just eighteen. 'He said he loved me – so, I married him.' The husband had seen her framed photograph on her father's desk in the law bureau, met her at a family dinner. The marriage had been a chance, too, to advance his career, by alliance with a wealthy lawyer's family. Now a black car and driver took him wherever he wanted. Advancements had come. His wife served her turn in the home. He came back late, tired from business. His wife waited up for him. On Saturdays the rich man lay in bed watching television all morning. 'Stay with me', he'd tell his wife. And she'd have to lie there too, hating the inanity of it all.

Then there were the parties by the pool. Rich associates would draw up in their large cars, fat Mexican wives would waddle up to the water's edge, with big diamond rings and earrings, arms heavy with jewellery. Others, more attractive, sat effacingly by, ornamental, while the successful men talked business. This was success. Wealth, the chauffeured car, the pool party, So what was wrong? Why did she suffer?

Now it was behind her. She stepped forward, her face small beneath a mass of black curled hair. Her eyes were brown with an uncertain light, sometimes vivid; her mouth was large, tentative and sensual at the same time. This was her yearly release. Only she knew she was not free. A thousand tiny bonds connected her to her husband. He paid for her here. He saw her off. He waited for her return. He phoned her to tell her about the children. She saw his face, above the immaculate cream suit and expensive leather shoes, as he stepped into the car to go to work. He did government work now. When there was a strike he would be hired to argue for the government with the men, persuade them to accept government terms. He could charm and be guileless, apparently. All this was richly rewarded. The Prime Minister had offered him the post of Ambassador to Belgium, but he had refused this. He didn't like it out of Mexico. The luxurious life, the house, had affected the woman's vision; what she saw was seen in its terms, the terms of her whole life.

The airport was crowded. Airports were part of her world, built for her. She was at home as she hurried through the immigration hall, waited for her baggage. She thought she must look nice as she handed her passport to the official and he smiled and waved her through. The world belonged to her and her class, literally.

On the terrace of the language school were set white tables. The sun shone warmly on the garden. There was a luxurious atmosphere of wealthy people at ease. A few young men sat idly on a low wall opposite, their white trousers neatly creased. Their sports shirts had designers' initials woven discreetly into the top pocket. There was an air of languid cash confidence about them. They knew they looked good. Their female counterparts sat also on the wall, or at the tables. These wore expensive dresses, rings and jewels. European, Middle Eastern, South American parents had sent their sons and daughters to be educated here. It was all a world of wealth, enclosed by walls with roses, resting in the sun. Nothing ugly came here. It was all paid for, the exclusion.

The woman sat. She was used to such surroundings. Wherever she went it was the same, the same rich places, the same immaculate people, the same smooth richness. Only there was the dissatisfaction in her. It was all so nothing. She was used to it. Idly she watched the young men on the wall. What were the bodies like beneath the clothes? The swimming and riding and exercise had formed the bodies well. But there was no glow from them. It was all too polished and bought. She had borne three children. But her own figure, she knew, was attractive. She wore a tight silk blouse, open at the throat, and cord jeans. There was a reserve about her; she saw the world with lurid personal criticism. But finally there could be no detachment. Her marriage bound her in firmly to the established forms, the smooth inflexibilities.

Then she saw a man approach a table near her. He sat down, rather angrily, she thought. He had dark hair, his eyes looked fierce and his frame was broad and heavy. There seemed a certain sadness about him, as if something wasn't right. He was rather casual about his appearance – he was turned in on himself. He made no effort to join in with the students. Rather he kept a field of isolating energy around himself. He interested her. She sat back, watching secretly.

The man sat looking at the garden. The flowers glittered harsh in the summer sunlight. His glance took in everything – he saw it all, quickly, the people on the wall, the girls. They were on the surface attractive enough. But he knew by now the poison it was all based in, the money origins. He watched the rich often as an obscene show. So many fathers, working in their rich organisations, so many loving daughters, rich sons, wild boys with money: it was so drearily known. Yet he was attracted in spite of himself. However it happened, these women were beautiful – some of them. Their clothes and jewels did enhance them. There was a heavy, tropical side to his nature, rarely expressed, that such people appealed to. In part he too wanted to be splendid, to shine out. Only some resistance obstructed him. The girls from the Middle East, with their black hair and melting dark eyes quickened his blood.

He saw the Mexican woman at the next table. She smiled slightly. He noticed her dark eyes that seemed slightly baffled, and the fulness of her form. But then he didn't associate himself with her. He looked back at the tall dark tree rising up in the centre of the lawn. The hum of rich voices was in the air; the afternoon light was hot and heavy. He was dissatisfied. He was here just to teach – to be the hireling of the ruling class. So, from underneath he could join in the superior world, see it, without the cash credentials normally required.

The bus ran swiftly along the blankness of the motorway. It was raining, and through the misted windows the man vaguely saw the fields lying across the western hills. The bus slowed down and turned into a service area. Rows of cars stood in parked lines. The place had no connection with anywhere: it stood isolated in the countryside. This was one social reality: the ordinary world. A few flags hung lifelessly from poles, in front of the concrete structure.

The students got off, interested in the new English place. And if it was a modern slum what did they care? It was a new sensation. In the background, modifying their vision, was the wealth of their own homes. How curious to mingle with these vulgar, badly dressed people. The Englishman too felt it was curious. How human it all seemed: the dreary people milling about, aimless, some playing on the electronic games machines. The foreign students were equally blank and aimless. Only, in their class, the aimlessness could take the form of expensive clothes, moulding the exterior form. They could spend, when they were bored. These others could only think of spending. A young Italian aristocrat inserted his coin into a game machine. A young English football supporter watched him. This was one of the few times the two worlds crossed. Wealth and poverty, side by side, spiritually inert both. But so different also.

The Mexican woman was borne in, among the crowd. She was passive, with two other Mexican friends. They all had rich husbands at home. She could be confident here, with the cash background always at hand. There was no risk. So she could be curious. But, with the self-effacement of the rich among the mass, she sat back and let the place exist around her. She knew she could detach herself whenever she chose. So, she could be indulgent, for the while.

The Englishman sat by himself, drinking coffee. The rain ran in grey rivulets down the windows high in the wall. He caught sight of the Mexican woman a few tables off. Her eyes in particular fascinated him. They looked gentle and mild. But that could be deceptive. His trust in things was breaking down. What did the externals signify? How did he know what was in her head? She could be quite vacant.

He didn't realise she also was looking at him. It didn't occur to him that he would figure in her landscape. He was jaded. The crowd moved along the counter, an ugly, shapeless mass. So what was there?

It was time to go back to the bus. He watched the Mexican woman go down the stairs. Her form seemed slight. What force was there in her? Wasn't it better to be alone, not to approach anyone? Only the energies forced him, moving him towards a woman. Outside the rain blew into their faces. A wind had started up. Paper cups blew about the blank tarmac and the flags rattled on their poles. A few people sat blankly in their cars, also.

The bus was running into the confused mess of outstretched London. It was best to switch off here, not to notice. Only he could never achieve this. The little houses, all so similar, a testament to the spirit of sameness inside, lined the roadway. A few women pushed prams about the empty pavements to the concrete shops. Outside, the air you breathed would be lifeless and sterile, flat. Imagine bringing children into this world, giving them this context. Everything seemed finished. His soul rose in energy against it all. But what else was there?

At the small hotel the students stood in the foyer waiting for their room numbers. It was below their usual level here. But, to go to such a place was novel to them. They could put up with it, as it was temporary. The woman stood in the group with three other Mexican wives. She looked clear cut, slim, as she stood there, faintly appealing. He moved over to speak.

'You are a teacher too, in Mexico, I think?' She turned to him with a brief smile, as if she had expected him to approach.

'Yes. At St. George's. But the rest of the time I am at home with my children.' Her large brown eyes looked softly and questioningly at him as she spoke. She liked this man. There was some contact between them. He watched her pass up the stairs to her room. This group of Mexican women: they seemed subjected, in a queer way he couldn't fathom. There was a kind of unconscious appeal they made in spite of themselves. He sensed their marriages were in some way imperfect. What force was it that made the appeal?

London was grey and hot. The cars piled past by the river. The galleries were to be visited. Inside the tall, stately building hung the canvases, to be admired. But there was no possibility of real admiration. The foreign students clattered round intent on consuming what there was to see. What could be more natural than this place to be there, for their benefit?

After all, the world was theirs, from Heathrow to Rome, to Jeddah, Tehran. The expensive hotels, clothes, cars, were at their disposal. So, if an artist painted, well then, his vision was theirs too, like a meal at the Hilton hotel. The kind of experience that might produce a picture was unavailable to them. Not that they actually saw anything – how could they, with such a cash vision – but they could imagine they were doing something important as they walked about.

He'd had enough. He left his group at last and went out of the building. There ran the Thames, grey and dead in the inert afternoon light. He would go back to the hotel. Down on the tube platform stood the rows of people. It was hot and stuffy. The train rattled in, the people got on. A few rich foreigners sat, with thick gold rings on their fingers, expensive clothes. The world was for them, if anyone: the servitude of the rest produced the means for these few to exist in material privilege. The train ran into his station. He got off.

It was peaceful, dark in the little room off the foyer of the hotel, arranged as a lounge. He sat there with the stifling air of London about him. It was pleasant just to sit. Lately he had become prone to fits of weird tiredness, as if his legs swayed and vision blurred. It was the stress of functioning amidst the sickness. Suddenly he was aware of a woman entering the room. It was the Mexican. She wore brown jeans, and a green silk blouse open at the neck, to reveal her brown flesh. She started slightly to see him there, and came to sit next to him. 'I was tired – so I came back.' She looked at him, rather wearily. He saw her eyes were tired, and that little lines ran from their corners, as if she'd been troubled. 'I was shopping – for my children. The others went on but I didn't like to. I don't like the shops.'

The man looked at her. 'Most of the students, that's all they like, shopping.'

'No, I don't like it. I hate it.' He eyed her again, interested. They sat for a few seconds, not speaking. 'How is your course?' He asked her gently.

'It's OK – only I don't understand it all.'

'I could help you – when we go back.' He wanted to establish some further point of contact. She smiled, in agreement.

'And tonight – what do you do?' She asked him.

'I don't know. Go out with the teachers, I suppose.' She had hoped he would go with her.

What did she want from him? He was attractive. But she wanted a deeper emotional contact. In Mexico her husband barely spoke to her. He did all he was meant to do. He went out, he earned the money, he gave her things. They were rich. She lived in a luxurious house. But there was nothing to it, no further life. And her imagination was stifling. Also, her body was held back. She had three children. But she had never desired her husband, not really. She had never felt the quick longing for him to touch her. There seemed no source of life in him she could reach for. He was all given over to the dead social purposes. She felt she had been tricked. She had been brought up to believe the man should do everything materially for the woman, that this was indeed the stamp and sign of his love. He was to be responsible. Only why was the responsibility so dreary? The social world was dead to her – she laughed and jeered at it.

But, in her criticism was still the allegiance and bondage to that world. She would be lost, she knew, without the luxury. She had formed habits and expectations dependent on it. So she was tortured, hating her state yet knowing she would never move out of it. It was this that made her so weary and depressed. There was no outlet. But this man, he seemed gentle, kind to something lost in her. She wanted to know him.

The weekend passed. On Sunday the course Director wanted to show the Mexican woman some sights in the city. He was a large, clumsy man who enjoyed the responsibility of six or seven women all dependent on him. He liked to imagine they all desired him. So they played a game together, them and him. It was raining; the bus swung round to pass the sights. It was all drearily predictable. What was the fascination, to see famous places? They were generally weights and oppressions on the free ground and air, places that should have fused away into nothingness. They were in a slow flux; in the end they'd vanish. But not fast enough. The teacher wanted it all gone, this society and its antecedent relics, cleared away. It was a mistake, an oppressive error. It made him sick to move about the streets. He sat in the bus, tired and by himself.

They got out to see the government buildings, the old

Abbey. It was still wet. 'Come under the umbrella?' The Mexican woman invited him. She slipped her arm through his. He felt the gentle sway of her breast against it. This was another bond, the contact. But over all there was still a weariness he could not dispel.

At the Abbey a long queue of people pressed up against the entry doors. They were all hoping to see something. What they actually saw, was obscure. It was as if the very capacity for seeing, for understanding, for intuiting, was dying out altogether, leaving only this collective non-vision. Were people really ceasing to exist, fading out? Yet they were there, assertive enough in the queue.

Inside the Abbey, he wandered with two women amongst the tourists. It was tiring to be there, so meaningless. The people pressed up in tight throngs, round tombs and pillars. What was needed was some new beauty, some new mark of truth for the present. This ghastly wandering amongst the sights of the past, all unseeing, was obscene. Yet who would bring to light the new life?

He liked to walk about with this woman, feel her close to him, near him. There was some tacit connection between them. He could imagine her life back in Mexico. He had no illusions about that, what it was. It was time to return. The coach was to collect the rest of the students, then head west, for home. On the way other sights were to be seen. He watched the woman again, climbing up a crowded street towards a castle, with her friends. She looked out of place, as if she withstood her context here, rather than enjoyed it. There was a kind of strain about her. Big planes flew overhead, heading west also. She belonged to their transatlantic world. Here was just a transit place. But also she felt a wistful affinity with England, almost a preference. However the pull of the known magnetised her, was too strong.

It was nearly dark when the bus turned in at the school gates. He helped her out with her luggage. 'Would you like a lift home? And tomorrow maybe we could meet?' He spoke politely but firmly. She smiled again. 'I'd like that. And you could give my friends a lift now too. They live where I do.' It was pleasant in the car in the hot evening, to drive with these women, home.

Afterwards he was thoughtful. He feared his life would have no proper form. He didn't want the usual things. There was to be for him no rising up in the job, no house, no marriage. Perhaps there could be the last thing. But what woman could he find who would relinquish her material interests? It was with a certain exultation he threw away the professional advantages. The whole edifice must come down. The society was dead. There could be no pretence, no evasion. It was all finished. Now all that remained was an aged edifice, painted up to conceal its age, made hideously strong by its hardened longevity. Everyone was so used to what was there. So the people streamed to work each day, blindly. And the repeats kept running; the thoughts, each day, repeated the previous day. It was all mechanism, actions habitual, thoughts the same. But the frame always dominated. For a man it was his work that he gave most effort to. He was there for most of the time he was awake. He could feel the virtue of doing something unpleasant for the sake of the wife and children, if he chose. Or else he could take a hard, cynical pleasure in his actions, in his rise. Whatever it was, his feelings were dictated by the frame. Nothing new came from him.

The women were the same. What did they expect, for the most part? That the man would serve them in the outer world. What did they care that it was dead and evil? It was his duty to support them. Or else, man-like, they became intact units, active themselves in the outer structures, immune.

It was a dreary sight. The essence of what the social norms were, appalled him. There was a destructive, self-wasting implication that made him vicious in resistance. The Mexican woman – he could see her in her home, wondering why she was so unhappy, so starved, in the midst of what was ostensibly the good life. There was the man, the husband, the important social figure. There were the house, the material goods, the comforts and badges of success. And there was she, the wife, not happy, though safe, provided for. What did she want? For a while she had liked it – the chance to adorn herself, dress up as a rich beauty. But it was all a sham and a sickness upon her.

It was the next evening. A gentle light stretched across the park; the sun had just gone down. Here on the edge of the small town the air seemed open to the further west. There was a freshness, a sense of anticipation in the evening. He walked up the hill slowly, watching the tall trees on the other side of the dark railings lift themselves up in black life. He rang the bell where she was staying. There was a distant barking of dogs.

She came to the door, rather shyly. She wondered what he would think of her. She half thought she was too old; there was little confidence in her. Only, she thought she looked nice also. She wore a light coloured blouse and jeans. She smiled at him – 'I was late, I had to hurry. What shall we do?' They walked down the pathway across the hilly park towards his car. In the distance big hills closed the town round; the sky was darkening and the air was fresh. There was a still coolness to the night.

'You know I am married?' She looked at him, anxious for his reaction. Perhaps he would dislike her for coming out like this. She felt partly guilty. But she knew also she would go back to her husband. And wasn't she entitled to do as she chose?

'Yes – does it matter?'

'Not really, except I feel guilty like this.' They reached the car. They would drive to a village nearby. She wanted to know about his life. He was conscious of her body as she spoke, as if she required something from him. All the time she was making an appeal. She seemed defeated in some way, turning to him for clarification.

They stopped at a pub near a canal. They sat in an upper

room, like an attic, with thick beams. A door was open, level with the canal. He could see the dark, still water outside. The cool air blew in. As she spoke, he watched her, noticing her eyes that looked heavy and sad. She wanted to tell him of her husband.

'He never talks to me – he doesn't care for me. I look after the children. He comes home late. And at the weekends he just rests – in bed, then by the pool. When we make love, it's nothing.' But it was clear she was held in some bondage by this man. What power did he have over her? He had financial power. And she bowed to this. In some way he was masterful, because he could manipulate the outer world so successfully. His chauffeured car, his government work, the smart suits, surely they were signs of something.

It was too far for her to leap, to discredit these things totally. As she spoke she was back in her house, moving amongst its fine fittings. She felt again his fish-like touch on her, pushed aside the full impact of her aversion to this good man. 'I don't like to think of it. So I make myself busy. And what can I do? He is a lawyer – if I ask for a divorce he can control the court judgment and take my children.' It was a relief to her, to tell these things to the younger man. She wasn't complaining. She spoke gently, wistfully, of what she had to tolerate. In her white blouse, against the wooden chair rest, with her black curling hair and heavy eyes and figure, she looked attractive. There seemed no centre of malice in her, no egotistic viciousness.

Only all her confidence was gone. 'I wonder, too, if I am a good mother. Sometimes I cannot stand to be with my children – to be just there, in control of them.' She was in an enormous trap; the initial error had got her there. She had accepted the man in marriage without thinking and the conventional patterns had closed her in, like a trap.

'So, why did you marry him?'

'I was young, and he said he loved me. And my father liked him.'

'What did you use to do – at the start?'

'We used to watch television, sit at home.'

'Didn't that make you wonder?'

'No, I thought if I loved him and he loved me, it didn't matter what we did.'

She opened up for him the curious vista of her past and present, feeling he could understand her. It was odd, he felt, how matter of fact about her life she was – she spoke of it calmly, as if she had often thought about these things.

'I tried to change it – to learn English, to teach at the school. And it's better now I can teach.' Even so the frame still held her, the rich fence around her vision. She could look through windows, even talk through gaps. But it wasn't possible for her to venture fully outside. 'I cannot leave him, because of the children.'

So there it was. Her life in the luxurious house, with its pool, its expensive fittings, would remain in all its imperfections. She would lock herself down emotionally, mentally and sensually for her children. Also she was not being completely honest. Because in her as well was a reverence for this man who brought her money and figured large in the outer world. So, despising and revering him both, she swung backwards and forwards.

She looked at the man from her dark, Mexican eyes. She reached across and took his hand. 'I like to watch hands. Yours are nice,' she told him. He let her stroke his arm gently. It was time to go.

They drove up into the hills, in the darkness. Beyond the ridge spread out the lights of the city. He stopped the car. She wanted him to make love to her. Partly she was trying to give herself what was deprived her for the rest of the year. And she liked this man, and his warmth. He seemed kind towards her. There was nothing lurid or sensational about the contact. She crept gently between his arms and lay there, her heavy breasts leaning against his chest, while he stroked her slight form. There was nothing exceptional in this – it felt natural. This was another centre of life. He felt his body stir with desire for her. Why shouldn't they gratify themselves?

'But I feel guilty. I was a virgin when I was married. And since then, no-one else has touched me.' What did it mean to her, being touched? What did it mean to anyone? It could be done in so many different spirits. So long as their egotism didn't catch hold of what they did, there could be no damage done. It should all take place in the darkness, out of consciousness. It was hard to reach this point. There was so much overlaying the honest, physical reality, to be got rid of. Her husband lay upon her like an incubus. She had borne him three children. She could not forget this.

Gradually, they drew back to consciousness, of where they were – of the lights burning in the valley. She looked at him, smiling. He wondered what she felt, what she could do with this experience. Was it just another glance through a chink in the rich fence, through which she could not slip? Where was he? Truly, the material world hardly existed for him. In his soul he felt always opposed and bitter with the outer forms. But perhaps his attraction to such a woman was a desire to sample the rich forbidden fruit. To steal in over the fence and take his pleasure with the rich man's wife – was this what he was doing? Or was the contact more real than that? Only their bodies could tell them. Was there a seethe of disintegration, a white light of going apart, of repulsion now between them? Or was there a richer glow, a new strength? If there was a new strength, it was all to the good.

He felt her presence warm beside him as he drove. She seemed in some way given up to him, moved. Only still her thoughts ran on her family.

'Perhaps I am bad, to do like this?' She looked to him for reassurance.

'Do you feel bad?'

'No, but when I think, I feel I am wrong.' She was ready with her mind to enclose and evaluate her feelings, to grind them small in the stones of orthodox morality. Only her breasts there in her blouse had another life of their own, that existed independent of her mind's control. If she chose she could kill her pleasure and her desire, lock it down. But why should she? He could do the same. It was odd how centuries of insisting on service, on duty, on righteousness left the body behind in some anterior, primitive zone. It was undiscovered, still its richness was to come forth.

He imagined her lying next to her husband in a bedroom that did its best to express the rich view of a sensual place. There would be pastel shades on the walls, on the lamps, on the bed covers. A few delicate chairs would stand neatly on a pink carpet. The chairs might be painted gold. The husband's beige suit would hang from a small, ornate handle of a white wardrobe. In the midst of all this she would be next to the man, while he touched her. This was the homely lair of the business man; this was where the rich man gratified his body. But amidst all the pastel tones the body was diffused also, and the passion, already bled away by the business deals and manipulations of the day, was a spent force. What did he look like naked, her husband? She didn't like to think of him. And had she let herself be bought, to be used there, in such a way, by such a person?

She was quiet as they drove on, back towards the town, thoughtful. 'So why is it wrong?' She wanted to know. 'I am also a mother.' But she could not deny the warmth that was now in her; her body felt rich and alive. He left her at her home. He would see her again tomorrow.

They met regularly. Each evening they would go somewhere, talk. There was a small restaurant, dimly lit, which they liked to visit. One Sunday afternoon, though, they planned to go out. It was hot. He drove up into the hills again, then swung off the main road over a cattle grid. The old estate spread out on each side of the tarmac drive. He liked it here, in this eighteenth century landscape. There were few visitors. The drive wound down a valley, through two steep hills with trees on their crests, to end up in a gravel yard in front of the mansion. There was a peace about the old place.

He wanted to show her the garden. They walked through the spacious hallway and through to the terrace beyond. Two peacocks walked on the lawns, while an old cat lay stretched out on the stone terrace floor. To the right high trees bordered the garden and enclosed it.

They sat down by the small lake where ducks were paddling. She leaned against him in the afternoon heat. This afternoon she was tired, older in appearance. She seemed to be worrying. He wanted to cheer her up. But he was a little remote from her; he knew soon she should go back. 'This morning my husband phoned me. My daughter, she's thirteen, she fell and broke her arm. And he says he misses me.' She looked down, as if communication with her family was unwelcome and oppressive. 'I wish I had no husband – no children.' She dug her hands into the grass with a tense movement. She didn't want to say any more. 'I would like to stay here – in this garden, with you.' Only it was just words. She knew she couldn't stay. The aspiration was real enough in spite of her knowledge.

She lay with her head on his stomach, looking at him out of the corner of her eye. She was quick to sense his moods. 'You are sad – what is it?' He didn't want to explain. There was a kind of futility about him, a background of disbelief. Would he go on and on like this, from incident to incident, with the main form of his life unchanged? He wanted to change it.

'Why is it we don't change – what stops us?' She looked at him sadly.

'I have my family, my children. I cannot leave them.' He didn't want to go with her. Who was it he could go with and where?

The big trees opposite burned in the sun. They grew up dense and sharply vertical, along the top of a high grassy bank. The garden was a bowl of warmth and freshness. The peacocks moved about the pathways, one following the other. The outer world was absent here. He felt the frustration grow inside him at the memory of the other; the peace here made it worse.

All at once he relaxed. He stroked her hair and looked at her, resting against his body. After all, it is good here, and the future could wait. So he tried to cheat himself. They rested there all afternoon. But a strong discontent was on him. Through her he saw another woman he wanted, as if she was a shadow of someone else he didn't yet know. He wanted a woman who was free of the material bondage – who could come forward wholehearted and warm to him. What good was it, to have contact and then return to the norm? It was a kind of cynicism. But she wasn't cynical – this was all she could allow herself. And when she was back in her house she would remember the afternoon with tenderness, and think 'yes, I was happy then.' But the rest of it would have to go on – the submission to the unwanted embrace, the caring for the children, the rich parties.

And this, he reflected, was how it was for most people. At the centre of their life was an unpleasant mainstream to which they submitted because they felt they had to. And out of this negative mainstream they tried to get temporary release. But always they went back to the central negation. It was like a madness. The process multiplied millions of times made up social life. He hated it. Why couldn't the central life itself be fine and decent?

It was getting dark. They would go back. As they drove she rested her hand against his leg. She knew, soon, she would be gone. But she liked this man, she would cherish fine memories of her time with him.

They were to meet in London, before she went back. The course ended. She was to spend a few days in the north of England. After that they would meet. It was still hot as the train pulled in under the wide arch of the station. He walked along the platform's grey length towards the barrier. He enjoyed it here, under the spacious roof. She was waiting for him.

Again she looked worn, as if the approaching departure was telling on her. She limped slightly. 'I tripped and hurt my ankle. So I nearly went back sooner. Only I wanted to wait, to see you.' They went into a small café near the station. It was hot inside, airless. She looked to him for some confirmation, after the few days of not meeting. He smiled at her. Only he felt himself uneasy for some reason he couldn't completely fathom. He didn't like it in the city, as if something extraneous was being forced on him. He was conscious of the thick miles of buildings round about, like a weight. He asked her about the trip north. She hadn't done anything in particular – just visited the usual sights in the towns. She looked defeated, as if something wasn't right.

'And tomorrow, it all starts again, the home, the children, the husband. And all the freedom ends for one more year.'

'You could change your conditions.'

'No, I can never change it. It is fixed. I couldn't leave the children.' She spoke dreamily, like a fated person reciting a doom. The children transfixed her, round them she rotated. In fact she saw the children as just her own – not really her husband's concern. But she was used to her life and even to its dissatisfactions; she was stabilised by the familiar links even when they restricted her. Only, at the same time, she longed for a different life. She must swallow her aspirations to this, when she went back.

The evening was desultory with the sense of impending departure. They went into a stuffy bar to drink. The place seemed run down, a refuge of a dying city. Litter lay on the floor, the paint was peeling. Here people came to enjoy themselves, gratify their beings in pleasure. What kind of being was it, that such a place befitted? He was down on it all.

There was a poignancy about her. She held her head sadly, in defeat. They went to eat in a small restaurant. He could see her wifely self emerging, unconscious. She was already back in her home. 'My husband – he will meet me, say how much he missed me,' – she mimicked his tone – 'and then all will be as before. I will get up at the same time, do the same things. Sometimes I drive fast, to have an accident, just for a change. But I can write to you and you can write to me.'

The man felt angry with her for having let her life be consumed in this way. Why couldn't she have waited, to marry someone she loved? But she had thought she loved the lawyer. Maybe love wasn't the point. Should she have married someone outside the norm, who could show her new ways? As a young girl, she had fixed on what she wanted. In her tentative, innocent way, she had resolved the material level she required in her marriage. Almost it was this she first thought of. Then the man fitted hazily in. She would love him. He was the master of the outer world, the sacred provider. She would be safe and adored. It also seemed that the very providing – of the house, money for fine clothes – was an act of adoration. She was like a queen, served and maintained. It was quite gratifying for a while. And the husband had adored her.

Only gradually, the social world took over. The huband's work came more and more to be his deepest gratification. There, in the service of the system, he derived his deepest pleasure. That world was real. He came home later and later. He provided on a more and more lavish scale. So, his wife could not say she was neglected. Thus he reasoned. And it was still an act of adoration for him to offer her the keys of the new luxurious home, show her the gardens, the pool, the fittings. All this – the fruit of his efforts. She must give him her approval and gratitude. He was also like a small child seeking sanction and reward for his activities.

Gradually, too, the deadness came upon her. She was subject to odd fits of depression, of sickness. The doctors could find nothing wrong with her. She had her children to care for, her home to run. But a kind of desperation was seizing her. She had all the time to shut down her awarenesses, cut them back. She could not afford to be self-conscious. And each year she would escape for one month or two, to England. But the mechanism that gripped her husband still enclosed her. She was never really free. Now she would return. Only now she realised she had missed something vital, made the wrong choice.

'But I am no good, not at anything. I cannot be an artist. I'm no good at being a mother, or a wife, I sometimes think. So what can I be?' She asked the question quietly; it was one she was always dwelling on.

'You could be yourself, a sensitive woman.'

'But I cannot be that. I have to care for my children, my husband, go shopping. And even my teaching, my husband doesn't like it. He never asks me what I have done. But I have to listen to him.' She was indignant. Fatally, also something submitted in her. It was the lot of women to submit, to put themselves aside. Who was she to be the exception, to have special needs? 'It would be better if I had never married. Only my single friends, they are not happy.'

'Maybe no-one is happy. But we can all try, to do what we believe.'

'I suppose so.' She looked at him, worried. They were a constant presence in her, these thoughts.

The meal was over. They passed out into the street. A big plane was climbing loudly through red stained clouds. It was a reminder of the next day. They would go back now, to the hotel.

The street was peaceful, transformed in the evening air, temporarily. Trees stood up at intervals, their dark green leaves dusty and heavy in the fading light. The hotel was small, set back from the mainstreet. 'Go to your room – I will come soon,' she told him. She was careful in case one of the other Mexican women would see her. She didn't want her husband to know anything.

He climbed the narrow stairs to the small room. The air was stuffy and hot. A table of charges was stuck onto the wall. He sat back on the bed. He heard her knock. She came in, quite shyly.

'Tomorrow – this time, I will be on the plane.' She watched him, sadly, trying to sense his reaction. He was sitting quietly, half-lying, in a reverie. She began to pull off her blouse, to offer herself to him. He noticed with a start that she was doing this. It was to be a final gift for him, before she went back.

She seemed child-like and small, though her figure was a woman's. She wanted to nestle against him, run her hands along his flesh. This was satisfying for her. He took off his clothes, slowly, rather awkwardly, as she lay there. It was strange to him, this meeting. There was something rather forlorn about her, as if she were sad. They lay back on the bed, passing into a darker unconsciousness. She needed him very much, to be like this with her, gentle and warm. It was a consolation to her, to feel him with her: the rest of her life was pushed to a distance. He felt her sadness in the way she yielded herself to him so pliantly. It was good, this movement and pleasure. Again there was nothing lurid about this meeting – it seemed natural. 'What time is it?' she asked him. 'Because I am sharing my room – I cannot stay all night.' She was afraid her friend might gossip about her. It was nearly two. She got up, reluctantly, to leave. 'I will wake you tomorrow.'

He heard her tap on the door. She was dressed in a bright white blouse and a skirt. She had bought the skirt for him, he knew. She kissed him shyly again. 'I will see you downstairs.' She was gone.

It was time to depart. He went to fetch a taxi. She sat with her arm through his, like one sentenced. But there was also a certain anticipation in her, for going back. It would be familiar for her there. 'My husband will wonder why I am wearing a skirt. I never wear one.' She wanted to play this symbolic trick on the Mexican man, as a defiance. To arrive wearing clothes chosen to please another man would be a kind of secret revenge. Her husband would never guess.

The taxi drew up at the London air terminal. It was

strange waiting with her to leave her luggage. Who was she, this woman he had talked to, been with for this time? What would she become at the far end of the journey? She would be a wife when she arrived. Her husband would move forward to claim her round the fence at the exit; moving amongst other Mexicans he would be the one her eye would single out by habit. And her life would begin again. His car would take her to their home. His money had bought it. There would be her children, her kitchen, her rooms. Only they had all come from him. She saw her husband clearly with the gleam of familiarity, recognised his suit, his movements. This was her world.

They sat on the coach together. She drew his arm against her so it moved against her breast. She liked to feel its pressure there. The bus was full of foreign people, in transit, returning. What did they all return to? There were so many separate worlds, apparently. But did they all revolve around the same principle? There were the inevitable men in expensive clothes, expensive women. How was the money earned? It was all the same system, the same mechanism, rewarding a few who worked it most efficiently, with the most. There were maybe people somewhere inside the clothes, with their hands on the handles of the cases. Only it was all a process of plausible masks and social functions. The reality of living hope was gone. He knew this as he looked about the bus.

The woman had no inkling of his thoughts. She felt the warmth of his body near her. It was reassuring. He had been nice to her. But the negative reality was drawing nearer.

The coach ran along a motorway packed with cars. On each side stretched out little meaningless streets, red brick houses, tall, blank flats, for the poor. Factories lay in ugly heaps at intervals. He watched the jets follow each other in, for the landing. What connection was there between the little red houses and the planes? The houses were at the bottom of the system; the smooth suited men on the bus paid no attention to them or their implication. Was this the best and fairest of all possible worlds, the best humanity could achieve for itself?

The coach turned up the airport approach road. They ran into the tunnel that would bring them up into the airport's centre. He was faintly excited and disgusted. A coil of roads wound in a circle between various tall concrete blocks. It was a functional place. But the ugliness was like a disease, a symptom. The rich men seemed to have spun this reality out of themselves; it was their essence laid bare and fixed down. Was this the cause of the narrow, mean spirit that prevailed? The men spun it out of themselves in evil self-expression. How was it all to be seen, after all? A man in a tailored suit, expensive shirt and shoes stepped past to get off the coach. What did it all mean to him, what vision did he have? He had long ago stopped seeing, his senses were gone and destroyed in the money motive. This woman, so fine and neat, what lay in her as she stepped off to follow the man? Jewels nestled beneath her ears, lay round her neck; her skirt was expensive and pleated. It was all of the best, a fair show. But from inside her apparatus what vision operated? Was there any sight left?

The Mexican woman bent forward to kiss him. She had no idea of his speculations. He was alone in these. She would never let herself go so far in condemnation. She was used to the airport. It was a means to an end. She couldn't see it for what it was. The face of things: this was what counted. So long as the face of things was fair, all could be vile and corrupt beneath. No-one should be allowed to lay bare the essence. This was the implicit social and human credo. She sensed he was unhappy. 'You think a lot. You should enjoy yourself more.' She wasn't stupid. But she didn't want to let herself be swamped with negative images. Enjoyment was the modern obsession.

They got off and pushed in through the glass doors of the terminal. Inside there was a mass of people queueing with cases, spreading into the cafés and shops. Sometimes a face of power and beauty would gleam across at him from a chair or a crowd. He was caught in an ambivalence. Why were so many beautiful women annexed by the cash world? He supposed under their faces and figures lay also the cash triviality, cash values. It was a waste.

They climbed up the stairs to the departure lounge. He was sorry she was going. Only could she survive in any other way but by going? She couldn't withstand the stress of full knowledge. She would never want to know it all. It was her limitation. But she had been fine and gentle with him, she had given him herself.

She wanted him to touch her, to stroke her gently. This was her consolation and evasion. She knew he was gone off somewhere, in his mind. She couldn't follow there. But his body was fine to her. And he had talked to her, helped her, understood her. What would become of him?

They sat drinking coffee. 'You would be a good father. You should marry, have children.' He smiled.

'Who should I marry? I don't meet anyone.'

'No, you are kind. You could find someone.' He wasn't so sure. In every woman seemed this ultimate bondage; in humanity there was a tacit conspiracy to see nothing, not to know. The face of things: well, there were even different ways of seeing a face. It hurt him to feel she wasn't with him in his perception. There was a fundamental sadness in him.

'Why do you think so much? Your body is good, fine. You do not seem like other men. You are warm and kind.'

There was no answer to give.

'You have to think,' he told her. 'There's no choice. Either awareness comes, or it doesn't. If it does, you put up with it.' She sensed his pain, the division between his warm bodily self and his vision which by instinct looked to the essence. Or was it just because of the warmth that he could see the essence?

'Let's go near the departure lounge,' he suggested. They sat near the entrance doors. She put her face forward to be kissed. She was crying a little. It was time for her to go in.

The doors swung closed behind her. She was gone, back to the old life. And where would he go, what would his life be?